PHENOMENAL PRAISE
FOR SEYMOUR WISHMAN'S
FASCINATING REAL-LIFE ANALYSIS
OF THE AMERICAN JUDICIAL SYSTEM

Anatomy of a Jury

"GRABS THE READER ON THE FIRST PAGE the way Raymond Chandler used to do, and it doesn't let go. Presents a boiling story of murder, sex, racial conflict, family tensions, and courtroom combat with that clear beauty of voice so rarely heard anymore: The hard, uncompromising ring of truth."
—*The Detroit News*

"THIS INSTRUCTIVE AND ENTERTAINING BOOK . . . should find its way into mystery lovers' libraries and law students' satchels alike."
—*Psychology Today*

"AN IMPORTANT NEW WORK."
—*The Los Angeles Daily [Law] Journal*

"A ROUSING ENDORSEMENT OF THE JURY and a superb description of how the system really operates."
—*St. Louis Post-Dispatch*

W9-CAH-365

QUESTION OF CONSENT

SEYMOUR WISHMAN

J

JOVE BOOKS, NEW YORK

QUESTION OF CONSENT

A Jove Book / published by arrangement with
the author

PRINTING HISTORY
Jove edition / May 1995

ISBN: 0-515-11608-4

A JOVE BOOK®
Jove Books are published by The Berkley Publishing Group,
200 Madison Avenue, New York, New York 10016.
JOVE and the "J" design are trademarks
belonging to Jove Publications, Inc.

PRINTED IN THE UNITED STATES OF AMERICA

10 9 8 7 6 5 4 3 2 1

To Samantha

QUESTION OF CONSENT

Prologue

IT WAS DARK when Lisa Altman left the theater that night. She left, as she always did after a performance, from the stage door at the side of the building. Only on nights when she premiered a new role were there crowds to meet her. This night was more typical. No one was there waiting—or so it seemed.

She walked down the narrow street toward Eighth Avenue. The other theaters' large marquees were as dark as her own. Their shows were also over, and their patrons were well on their way home.

Long before Lisa heard any footsteps, she sensed there was someone there. It was a kind of intuition she sometimes had when she felt a person staring at her out of a large group of people in a theater; the entire audience may have been watching her dance, but the others were somehow looking with less intensity. Whenever Lisa felt this unnatural stare coming from one person in the audience, she would be able to locate him almost instantly. Invariably it was a man, and it always unnerved her and made her more self-conscious as she danced. It didn't happen often, but it always gave her the creeps. And it was never her imagination.

Now, as she walked down the street, she knew someone was watching her, and she felt her body tightening. She looked over her shoulder. No one was there . . . that she could see. She quickened her pace, reached the corner, and headed up Eighth Avenue. For the next several blocks she walked faster than she usually did. She passed some hookers waiting for work, a porn theater, an all-night deli, some more hookers. No wonder the neighborhood was called Hell's Kitchen.

She crossed over to the west side of the street, and as she did so she noticed, about a block behind her, someone else crossing the street. She was right—there was someone behind her. She walked faster. Another block and she reached the male porn theater on her corner and turned. She didn't need to look. She knew the man was following her.

Her street was dark. One of the streetlamps was out. It had been out for days. "Damn the city," she muttered. The rows of four-story brownstones on either side of the street gave off little light. She had reached the middle of the block when she first heard his footsteps behind her, following her. If only she could make it to her building, she would be safe. Each step made her more anxious, more afraid.

She reached into her large black leather tote bag to get out her keys so that she wouldn't be delayed in opening the front door. The keys were at the bottom of the bag. She fumbled through the ballet shoes, the tights, the sweatshirt. She found her purse and pushed it aside. She kept walking, not slowing her pace. Her hand fluttered around the bottom of the bag. Finally, she found the small silver ballet shoe on her key chain. She grabbed the keys as she reached the stoop of her house. She raced up the nine steps to the front door, pulling the keys out of the bag as she ran.

She made it to her front door. She was almost safe, almost home. She searched for the right key, the large one with teeth on both edges. She found it and slipped it into the lock. She turned the key and pushed the heavy wooden door open. She stepped inside the vestibule and swung the door back. It was too late. He was standing immediately behind her.

He shoved the door toward her.

Lisa stepped back.

"I'm not going to hurt you," he said. He was dressed well—fine overcoat, suit and tie, expensive hat.

"What do you want?"

"I was hoping we could speak for a few minutes," he said in a soft, almost apologetic way. He looked over at the five mailboxes, each with a number, a name, and a bell underneath. There was her name, "Altman," and under her name the number 1.

The keys dangled from her hand. She stood motionless, frozen, as if the music in a pas de deux had stopped and it were her partner's turn to dance alone.

"Open your door," he said softly.

She walked a few steps down the hallway and turned to her door. She slipped the key into the lock and opened it.

"Go inside," he said.

Lisa obeyed. She was frightened. Without really thinking, she stepped inside her apartment. Yes, she should have screamed, or run, or hit him in the groin with her heavy bag. But without knowing why, she merely obeyed.

Part I ⚖

Chapter 1

THE CRIMINAL COURTHOUSE at 100 Centre Street in downtown Manhattan was a massive structure, with two entrances in the front and windows—tall and narrow like gun slits—running up the side of the building.

A wooden rail separated the trial participants in the well of the courtroom, which took up the front third of the room, from the crowd of spectators seated in the rows behind the rail. Twelve regular and two alternate jurors were in the jury box, intently studying the witness.

I stood on the opposite side of the courtroom, near a window, leaning back on the wooden rail, about thirty feet away from the witness. I had stood there through most of the direct examination, occasionally looking out the window, not taking notes, with my arms folded across my chest. I certainly would not have appeared to the jury to be particularly impressed with the testimony or anxious about the time a few moments from now when I would cross-examine the witness—and that was, of course, exactly the impression I wanted to leave.

It was just another trial, or so it had seemed to me at the time, and Lisa Altman was just another victim . . . or alleged victim. She might have been telling the truth, or she could just as easily have been lying—it didn't matter to me. All I knew for sure was that I was doing my job, defending my client the way I was supposed to, trying to win yet another case. And when it was my turn, after the prosecutor had finished with her, I would try to destroy her.

The acoustics were lousy. Not much sound bounced off the lowered ceiling in the courtroom, making me strain to hear every word. But I managed to catch every nuance, without appearing anxious.

The fluorescent lights were too bright. A glare bounced off the imitation marble wall behind the witness so that if I stared too long, the witness's image jumped out at me. I periodically focused on the beautiful, twenty-nine-year-old woman in the witness chair. I would hold my gaze on Lisa Altman for a few moments, then look away.

Newspaper reporters were in the first two rows of the spectator seats, more reporters than I'd ever seen at one of my trials before—but of course, Lisa was an international celebrity. The thought occurred to me that if *I* were one of the world's greatest ballet dancers, known for brilliant interpretations of tragic roles, I would probably get this kind of turnout on a regular basis.

The reporters looked more skeptical than the rest

of the audience, but then, they usually did at my trials. On balance, the press treated me well, although I would have been happier if they had called me "ruthless" a little less often.

Judge Richard Bennett was on the bench. I had been in his court many times before. Some judges insisted on controlling every aspect of a trial, but Dick Bennett would let the lawyers try their cases without interfering too much in their cross-examinations. With his graying temples and bright blue eyes, Bennett was a commanding presence in the courtroom. But there was little he could do to protect the witness from me. On the other hand, the judge was a tough old bastard, and I knew that if the jury convicted my client, Bennett was certainly going to send him to the clink for a long time.

The court clerk was working on a crossword puzzle at his desk in front of, below, and to the right of the judge. The court reporter was silently typing into her little machine at her place in front of, below, and to the left of the judge.

The prosecutor, John Phalen, was seated at counsel table, taking Lisa through the direct examination. John was in his late thirties, with wiry, thinning hair that he brushed carefully to make it look fuller. He wore the basic polyester, double-knit suit so popular among law enforcement authorities.

The defendant, William Betz, was at the other end of counsel table, next to my empty chair.

The prosecutor should not have been seated. He should have been standing at the far end of the jury box. I always stood there when interrogating one of my own witnesses. That guaranteed that in answering my questions, the witness spoke loudly enough for the whole jury to hear. By standing behind the jury, I also forced the witness to face the jury and establish some eye contact.

I knew I would begin my questioning of Ms. Altman almost playfully, as I slowly tried to gain control over the length and tempo of her answers. Gradually I would gain control not only of the responses, but of the witness herself. I would dominate her, beat her, humiliate her, and finally dismiss her—at least that was my intention.

"Your witness," the prosecutor announced.

I watched one of the newspaper artists drawing with pastels. I recognized myself on the pad—the long, narrow nose, the slightly messy hair, the accusing finger pointing at Lisa Altman in the cross-examination that was about to begin. Lisa looked very attractive in the drawing. The artist, however, could have been a little more generous toward me. He looked up and winked at me.

"Your witness," the prosecutor said again.

I scanned the jury. Mostly women, they waited expectantly. I preferred to have women on the jury when another woman was being judged. For Lisa to be lying she would have to be moved by cruelty and spite. And women, I felt, were very good at understanding cruelty and spite. Women were more suspicious, less accepting, more vindictive. I didn't care whether Dr. Orloff, my shrink, thought my view of women jurors was distorted.

"The jury a lawyer picks looks like the inside of his own neurotic head," I had recently joked at a cocktail party. But deep down inside I really didn't include myself as one of the "neurotic." I won most of my cases, and that should have been proof for Dr. Orloff that my jury choices weren't neurotic.

"The witness is yours, Mr. Roehmer," Judge Bennett said. He leaned back, his head resting on the bump of a pillow on top of his black leather chair.

I nodded to the judge. I'd heard the prosecutor, but I wanted to build some anticipation before beginning. I took several menacing steps toward the witness.

I was well aware that all eyes in the courtroom were focused on me. The jury was composed of twelve critics to be persuaded; they watched my every movement. Spectators had filled the courtroom to cheer their favorite players. The witness, the client, the court attendants, the court reporter taking down every word—all were there to see and appreciate. God, there was much that I still loved about trials.

Lisa Altman sat with her legs crossed—well-defined, muscular legs. Her hands rested, one over the other, palms up, on her lap; she had long, lovely fingers. She wore a handsome brown tweed suit. Her blond hair was pulled tight in a bun behind her head. Her eyes were fixed on me—pale gray, cold eyes conveying a self-possession, a confidence, that seemed to me a kind of bravado intended to challenge me. We both knew I had to break her to succeed, and although I might have been imagining it, I sensed, in the slight tilt of her head, a dare. But at the same time, I could feel a vulnerability beneath that affect of defiance.

I began with my hands in my pockets, my weight evenly distributed. "You said on direct examination that you make a living as a ballet dancer," I said in a casual, conversational tone, my eyebrows arching upward. "Did you ever study acting?"

"Yes," Lisa Altman answered quickly.

I immediately sensed her tension. That would make it easier. The nervousness would create the impression she was evading or lying.

"Wouldn't you say that you're acting while you dance?" I spoke slowly. I always tried to speak slowly in front of a jury.

She shifted stiffly in her chair. "Yes."

"About how many hours a day do you practice?"

"Eight, ten hours. But most of that is simply physical exercise, not acting." Lisa must have known— with good reason—that traps were being laid for her by this professional manipulator who knew all the rules.

"But surely much of that is rehearsing performances?"

"Yes, of course."

"And you practice five, six, sometimes even seven days a week, don't you?"

"Yes."

"In fact, you've received excellent reviews for your acting abilities, haven't you?"

"Yes."

"Why, you've been called one of America's most expressive, most convincing dancers, haven't you?"

"Yes."

I knew that the courtroom was a very different theater, and that her acting abilities in this arena hadn't been tested yet. Mine had been. I smiled. "Yes, you're very good."

"Objection," John Phalen said from his seat at counsel table.

"I withdraw the remark. But I did want to ask," I said, maintaining my focus on the witness, "how many performances have you given so far in your life? Hundreds, would you say?"

"Yes, hundreds," she said defiantly.

I liked beginning in an unexpected area. If I could rattle the witness, I knew I had an edge on the rest of the cross-examination. And since there was no risk in these questions, I could, at the very least, get a feeling of how she'd move. I was already pleased. Her short answers were a good sign. Eventually she would try to lengthen her answers with explanations, but I sensed I could set a pattern of short answers that I would be able to force her back to later. Dominating a witness meant limiting and controlling all responses.

"In fact, you performed on stage the night after the incident in question, didn't you?"

"Yes."

"Now, you said on direct examination that you never met the defendant before that night, isn't that correct?"

"Yes, that's correct.

"Never met him backstage or anywhere else, correct?"

She hesitated. "Yes."

I could see that the jury sensed she wanted to say more. Since the line I was pursuing wasn't crucial to my attack and since I wanted to avoid giving the impression I was trying to trick her, I backed off. "Did you want to improve that statement?"

"Well, actually, I do remember about a week before that night, after a performance, he pushed into me backstage. But we didn't actually meet."

I shook my head disapprovingly. "Now, now, Ms. Altman, my question was—didn't you *say* on direct examination that you never met the defendant before the night of the alleged incident?"

"Perhaps I was being too literal. But we didn't really meet."

"So the defendant had bumped into you prior to that night?"

"Yes."

"Have my questions been helpful to you in jogging your memory?" I asked, almost playfully.

"Perhaps I was too literal. It was a misstatement."

"Do you remember making the same, how shall we say, 'literal misstatement' to the grand jury? Do you remember saying to the grand jury"—I read from my transcript—" 'No, I never met him before that night'? Do you remember saying that, Ms. Altman?"

"I guess I do. Yes."

"You were under oath when you testified before the grand jury, weren't you, Ms. Altman?"

The witness nodded.

"You have to answer out loud so the stenographer can take it down for the record. What is your answer?"

"Yes," she said, leaning forward a bit.

"Then the statement before the grand jury was"—I pretended to grope for a phrase—" . . . a literal misstatement also, wasn't it? Because now you admit that you did, in fact, see the defendant as recently as a week before the incident."

"No, I don't remember being asked."

I walked over to counsel table. "Permit me to refresh your recollection," I said. I searched through several books of transcripts waiting in a pile on counsel table. I came to the one I was looking for and flipped the pages to the passage I wanted. I walked slowly over to Lisa with the book in hand. She reached for it. I slowly pulled the book away. Lisa watched me, observing every movement I made as I walked in front of the witness stand. I could tell she was a woman who didn't like to be teased.

"When you said 'backstage,' I remembered him pushing into me. I told him to watch where he was going."

"Then you not only saw him, but you admit speaking to him at that time?"

"I spoke to him. I told him to watch where he was going. That's all I said."

I smiled. "Yes. You saw him and spoke to him. You now admit doing both after twice swearing you did neither."

The courtroom was quiet. I stood in front of Lisa with my arms outstretched. I studied the witness as she stared at me. The two long muscles at the front of her neck were taut.

Although my approach to cross-examinations varied with each witness, I knew the experience of testifying was almost always terrifying. No matter how relaxed Lisa pretended to be, she had to be nervous.

She had to abide by the rigid rules of the court, although she had not been informed of these rules in advance. *I* knew the rules. She didn't have a script or choreographer's plan. She had no control over events as she was scrutinized by a jury and an intimidating, robed judge looking down on her. *I* had control over the events of the "cross." I could yell at her, shoot rapid-fire questions, be sarcastic, or accuse her outright of being a liar. I didn't know if Lisa was telling the truth. It was simply my job to make her appear to be lying. That's what any criminal lawyer worth his salt would have seen as his job.

As time passed and the cross-examination continued, Judge Bennett sat passively, patiently, as he had to, waiting. If ever I slipped and gave him the opportunity, the judge would slam me in front of the jury. But I was being careful. I might risk contempt when the jury was out of the courtroom, but in their presence I was respectful of the judge. With my remark about Lisa's acting skills, I had almost gone too far, but not quite, and I had withdrawn the comment right away. I doubted the judge had expected me to be aggressive like that so soon. No, the only function for Judge Bennett, patient Judge Bennett, was to wait. The judge must have felt frustrated and angry at his inability to help the witness. Lisa Altman was going through the first stages of a process she would not be able to control, and the judge had to accept that she was in my hands. Poor Judge Bennett couldn't do anything for her. He, too, had to play by the rules.

It was fifteen minutes into the cross, and I had planted myself ten feet in front of the witness. I stood directly between Lisa and John Phalen, blocking her view of her only sure ally in the proceedings. John didn't realize how isolated a witness could feel. I would never have abandoned one of my own witnesses like that.

"You *sensed* him following you?" I was asking my questions with directness, the conversational tone long gone.

"I felt his presence," Lisa responded immediately. "It was dark and I only saw his shadows in the darkness." The veins bulged blue on the back of her left hand as it smothered the fist of her right. I, of course, noticed that, and it pleased me.

"You heard him?" I didn't care how she answered. I wanted a rhythm, a rhythm of my questions and her answers, a rhythm of me demanding and her relenting. I would get her to shorten her answers; then I would have her.

"I heard his footsteps behind me, following me. I felt . . ."

"Did you try to run?" I knew she had told the police that she had walked directly home without calling for help.

"I was too frightened to run. I felt somehow that would anger him. I don't know why. I guess . . ."

"But you were in excellent physical condition from exercising sometimes ten hours a day, seven days a week, isn't that true?"

"Yes."

"Yet, you didn't run?"

"No, I didn't run."

"Did you cry out for help or go for a cop?"

"I was too nervous. I wasn't thinking."

"You didn't call for help?"

"I sensed that for some reason it was just between

the two of us. I was just trying to get away. I didn't think of anyone else."

"You went straight for your apartment?"

"It was my home."

"You led him straight to your apartment?"

"I wasn't 'leading' him anywhere. I thought I'd be safe there."

"You unlocked the front door, and you both entered the building together?"

"I thought I would be safe there. It was my home." Lisa coughed, then coughed several times more.

I turned to the court officer standing by the window. "Could the officer bring the witness some water? She seems to be having some difficulty."

"If the witness is having any difficulty, she can ask me for water. She seems to be doing fine," Judge Bennett said.

"Actually, Judge," Lisa said, "I *would* appreciate some water."

The judge nodded, and the court officer went into a back room. Everything hung silent in the courtroom; all action was suspended. I turned to the jury as they studied the witness. I knew Lisa didn't need water; I didn't care if she did. I was pleased that some jurors would probably take her request as a stalling tactic to give herself time to think about her answers. I had asked for the water so I would appear considerate as I headed into the hardest part of the cross. Bennett knew that I didn't give a damn about the witness, and I also didn't give a damn about what Bennett thought.

I turned around and surveyed the courtroom. Several of the spectators were familiar to me. They were old men and women who had attended earlier trials of mine—particularly the sex cases—mostly retired people with time on their hands. Criminal justice to them was live soap opera. I'd had short conversations with a few of them over the years.

The court officer emerged with a glass of water and handed it to Lisa Altman. As I walked past, I said in a soft voice, but loud enough for the jury to hear, "Thanks, Tony."

Lisa took a few short sips. She was breathing hard.

"Are you better now, Ms. Altman?" I asked.

"Yes, thank you," she said, forcing a smile that might have looked natural from the back of a theater.

"Can we go on?"

"Yes." She sat erect, with her shoulders pushed down and her head held high, accentuating the long, dignified neck.

"We left off where you opened the door for him," I said.

"I *didn't* open it for him. He ordered me to open it," she said, speaking with anger, but straining to retain her odd smile. Lisa's eyes seemed to concede to me that her delay had gained her nothing. There was no course but to give in to my control over the moment, and over her.

I had felt that point of resignation with other witnesses, and it always unleashed in me a new surge of energy.

Sometime later in the cross I was shooting the words at her. "He threw you on the bed?" I said, taking several steps toward her. I had decided to risk bringing out the most damaging part of her testimony under direct examination again. It would be worth it if I could get what I wanted in the end. If there was no payoff, the worst evidence would be reinforced in the jury's mind. The gamble had to work.

"Yes, he did," Lisa said, her inappropriate smile still set.

"He ripped off all your clothes?"

"Yes." She moved back in her chair.

"He lay on top of you?" I leaned closer to her.

"Yes, on top of me."

"He pushed his knee between your legs?"

"Yes."

"You struggled?" I felt my domination of the room, of the witness.

"Yes, I struggled," she answered feebly.

I stepped directly in front of her, a foot away. "He entered you?"

"Yes."

"You struggled?" I said loudly.

"Yes, I struggled."

"You moved under him?" I yelled.

The muscle around Lisa's mouth began to quiver. "Yes," she said, pushing her body into the back of the chair.

"You wrapped your legs around him?"

"Yes. Yes, I wrapped my legs around him," she said, losing control.

"He reached an orgasm?"

"Yes."

"You came?" I said softly.

Lisa tried to catch her breath. Her eyes bulged.

"Objection! Objection!" John Phalen said, leaping to his feet. "This woman is not on trial here. It doesn't matter how her body responded . . ."

As John Phalen continued to make his objection, Lisa and I stared at each other. Both of us were trying to regain our composure from the excitement of the encounter. "I wrapped my legs around him." That was as good as a confession, I thought to myself.

Neither of us heard Judge Bennett sustain the prosecutor's objection and admonish me.

Lisa was trying to take deep, even breaths.

I pushed my hair off my forehead and stepped back a few feet from the witness. Admitting her orgasm would have been *signing* the confession, I thought to myself. I could feel the sweat from my armpits run down the sides of my body.

"When it was over, you stopped struggling?" I asked in a softer tone.

"Yes. I stopped struggling. It was over. He just left."

"You weren't just acting when you were struggling, were you?"

"No, I wasn't acting."

"Are you sure? Because you did admit being aroused by it all."

"Objection. She never admitted any such thing," the prosecutor said.

"But in effect she did admit it, Judge. And I was curious to know if she'd concede the possibility that—at least unconsciously—the struggling was only an act."

"Sustained! And I don't want to warn you again, Mr. Roehmer. You know your questions are improper. Restrain your curiosity."

Ignoring the judge, I turned back to Lisa. "As one of America's most expressive dancer/actresses, as the critics call you, you're very aware of the effect of your performances on your audiences, aren't you?"

"To some extent, yes."

"But you had no idea that you were having an effect on the defendant, no idea that you were provoking him, leading him on? His interest in you came as a total surprise?"

"Objection."

"Withdrawn."

Lisa Altman's lips were dry and slightly parted, and her eyes seemed to me faintly glazed as she stared at my chest. It was now apparent from her appearance that I had succeeded in destroying her. I looked at her with contempt. "You waited a week before making a criminal complaint?" I asked.

"I didn't want to make a complaint. I wanted to forget about it. I didn't want to have to face a trial like this."

"You knew his name because it was sewn into the raincoat he left at your apartment. Is that correct?"

"Yes, that's correct."

"Did you think it strange that the man you claim raped you left, as it were, his calling card in your apartment?"

"He ran out when he had finished with me. I didn't think it was strange. I thought it was disgusting."

"Didn't you say on direct examination that you delayed filing a complaint not because you wanted to forget about it but because you thought the publicity would harm your career?"

"Yes, that too. There were two reasons."

"Two reasons, you say . . ." I paused, reviewing in my mind what I'd covered. Another few thrusts and I would be ready to close the cross. I had learned long ago the delicate balance between successfully exploiting a moment and, by going too far, either losing control of the witness or generating sympathy for her with the jury. I made the judgment of when or where to stop by relying on an intuition that told me how much was left in a witness and what kind of impression was being made on the jury.

"The clothes, your torn clothes, do you at least have those to show us?" I asked disdainfully. I knew from the pretrial discovery supplied by the state that she hadn't kept them. I was taking no risks now.

"I threw them away that night."

"You don't claim that the defendant had a weapon, do you?"

"No."

"You did not receive lacerations?"

Lisa shook her head.

"You did not receive any lacerations?"

"No."

"You did not receive any contusions?"

"No."

"You didn't go to a doctor, did you? There wasn't even an internal medical examination, was there?" I knew there hadn't been one.

"No. No, there wasn't. I just washed up. That was all I could think of doing. I just washed up."

I stared at the witness. She tried to return my gaze. I could see her struggling to look me in the eye, to show me her remaining strength. I knew she was fighting against lowering her eyes, to avoid admitting that I had beaten her. I felt exhilarated as I glowered at her. Lisa looked away.

"There is nothing more of this witness," I said, leaning against the wooden rail about thirty feet from the witness stand.

Lisa stepped down from the witness stand and walked past me. She glanced at me and quickly turned away. She was not as tall as I had thought on first seeing her, although she now seemed more beautiful, more feminine. She walked to the row of benches behind the reporters and sat down. Her face looked flushed. Breathing heavily and appearing shaken, she began watching me—more in fearful anticipation than in anger, it seemed to me.

As her stare fixed on me, I felt a new wave of strength coursing through my body, as if another round of the cross were about to begin. On balance, the questioning had gone as well as planned, I thought. Maybe even better.

I returned to my seat at counsel table and sat down next to my client.

William Betz leaned over. "That was terrific," he whispered to me. He patted me on the forearm.

I smiled at my client reassuringly—or so it would have appeared to the jury. "Take your fucking hand off of me. Don't you ever touch me again," I said, speaking softly so that the jury would not hear my anger and self-contempt.

Chapter 2

THE FOLLOWING MORNING I began my summation, as I usually did, by citing the state's burden to build with solid bricks proof beyond a reasonable doubt. I spent most of my two hours pounding the prosecutor's bricks with a battering ram consisting of accusations of inconsistencies, implausible coincidences, and "literal misstatements." In cases I considered weak, I shouted, but here I never raised my voice.

By the conclusion of the summation I was speaking in a near whisper. "It would be more satisfying to all of us if we could understand why a woman like this would provoke and manipulate. Perhaps it was some perversion, or masochism, or lust, or hatred of men—who knows? She may not know herself. But the law recognizes the difficulty of fathoming people's motives, and therefore imposes a burden on the alleged victim to convince you that she did not provoke the intercourse. She must prove to you beyond a reasonable doubt that she did not consent to it. Although the defendant has no such burden, we did show how my client was the manipulated victim of this tough and calculating woman.

"If it comes down to her word against my client's— and I think it does—you must give my client the benefit of any reasonable doubt. If she had sustained wounds and had photographed them, or if she had torn clothes she could have shown us—if there were any corroboration beyond her own testimony—we would have a different case. For you to find a person guilty, you must be convinced by hard evidence from the state. Too much is lacking here."

The last line of the summation was like the last line of all my summations, reminding the jury of their oath, "in the name of God, to well and truly try the case." Summations were easy.

When the prosecutor began his summation, I sat expressionless. Beyond this point in the trial I could no longer address the jury—not directly, anyway. "Mr. Roehmer told you all morning about reasonable doubt," the prosecutor said. "But you have to accept what Judge Bennett tells you it is, and he will tell you that everything in human affairs is subject to some possible or imaginary doubt, and a possible or imaginary doubt is not *reasonable* doubt. . . ."

I sat waiting. I had heard so many summations. During my first jury trial I had nervously written down every word. Now it was an effort to pay attention. At least those parts of the trial in which I was performing still excited me. And I was very good when I got excited.

My father had sold life insurance, mostly to working-class people who couldn't afford it. He would have been impressed by my performance in this trial, impressed that I had never lost my focus on the jury as my "customers." My gentle, adoring mother would have been thrilled by how self-assured and decisive I'd been. Both of my parents had been dead for years: they had died while I was still in law school.

My darling daughter, Molly, would have been proud of all the respect and attention I was receiving— Molly was four years old. My ex-wife, Jenny, would have been appalled. She had divorced me about a year earlier. After twenty-two years of living together. Easy come. Easy go.

". . . The defendant does not deny the intercourse . . ." the prosecutor shouted. There was no reason for the prosecutor to shout about this point. The intercourse was undisputed. Consent was the issue, and the jury understood that. Hysterics only made the jury more suspicious. The prosecutor should have saved his outrage for the part of the case that touched on the issue of force. I should win the case on its merits, I said to myself, but this guy is helping.

During my first year out of law school I had clerked for a criminal trial judge, Lloyd M. Singer, a gentleman of humor, intelligence, and decency. Every day in the course of his trials, "Bear," as Judge Singer was affectionately called by his friends, made decisions based on his deep sense of fairness. I remembered, as the prosecutor continued his summation, that there had been nothing I'd wanted more than one day to be a man of such integrity and conviction as my judge.

Defending Betz didn't, at this moment, strike me as ennobling work.

Bear had urged me to become a prosecutor after my clerkship with him. And that's what I did, trying one case after another. And I learned my trade and loved what I learned. As far as the defendants I prosecuted were concerned, they were all guilty, I was sure.

The prosecutor went on: ". . . A woman's obligation to resist ceases once overcome by force or fear, even prior to when penetration of her body is finally consummated."

I suppressed a smile as I tried to imagine what the last incoherent garble would read like when the puzzled-looking court reporter transcribed her notes.

"Why should this woman come to court and perjure herself?" It was John's strongest argument, and I had been waiting for it.

"Objection!" I screamed, jumping to my feet. "This is improper comment. It implies a burden of proof on the defendant. The woman admitted satisfying her lust. The defendant can't explain her behavior afterward, and doesn't have to."

"Overruled," Judge Bennett said. "You've had your summation, Mr. Roehmer. The jury is admonished to disregard Mr. Roehmer's remarks. Let's go on."

I sat down, satisfied. I'd had no chance of winning with such an objection, but I knew the jury was incapable of putting my impassioned remarks out of their heads. The judge I had clerked for would have been outraged had I grabbed for this kind of little advantage in a trial before him. He used to call a lawyer who knowingly made improper statements in front of a jury "an edge grabber," and he would hold the lawyer in contempt if he did it again in his courtroom.

The rage I had exhibited during my objection slowly faded as John Phalen plowed on. I never actually lost my temper in a trial unless I wanted to. But as contrived as those displayed emotions were, when I acted them out they were real to me, as real as anything in my life. That was why juries usually believed me. They had believed me for almost twenty years as a defense lawyer pleading for acquittals, and before that they had believed me when I had been a prosecutor pleading for convictions.

Judge Bennett delivered his charge to the jury in a dry, flat tone, as if he were reading some bloodless, boring statute like the Mechanic's Lien Act. Bennett's tone and the familiar words of the general instructions—"the obligations of jurors . . . reasonable doubt . . . evaluating testimony" and on and on— were numbing to me. But two of the jurors were leaning forward, cupping their hands behind their ears. Wonderful institution, the jury, I thought.

I felt my mind slip into a kind of automatic pilot, relying on reflex to catch variations from the standard charge. Resting my chin on my fist, I drew on my yellow legal pad a series of little stick figures hanging from little stick scaffolds. Bennett charged on. I didn't expect to lose, but drawing the little hanging men amused me, while my anxious client leaned over, as I had known he would, to look at my notes.

After two years of prosecuting cases I had decided that I no longer cared about getting people convicted and sent to prison. I believed at the time that I wasn't sufficiently engaged in what I was doing. Sure, I had still wanted to win, but that was simply because I always hated to lose anything. Things would be different when I was a defense lawyer, I had thought. The object of the game would be to keep people *out* of jail. That would be worth the fight.

At some point, some unnoticed point well before the cross-examination of Ms. Lisa Altman, I had finally given up—for reasons I didn't yet understand—the illusion that there was a moral component in my work. Skill, sure, but anything nobler was just plain bullshit.

Finally Bennett got to the specific instructions defining the crime of rape. I put my pencil down and tried to concentrate. This was the most important part of the charge, and Bennett dropped the pretense of not reading his notes.

"If a woman assaulted is physically and mentally able to resist, is not terrified by threats, and is not in a place and position that render resistance useless, it must be shown that she did, in fact, resist the assault. . . ."

Leaning back, I looked over to my right at my client. The defendant sat with his legs crossed, his sweating, short-fingered hands folded in his lap, his shoulders raised and pushed back. He must have thought he looked relaxed. I knew the jury couldn't see the man's chest pumping those short, quick breaths.

I was always aware of the way I looked to juries. I wanted to appear comfortable with myself—earnest, sincere, and, above all, honest—more interested in the substance of my cause than appearances. I always wore simple gold-rimmed glasses and traditional penny loafers, and, unlike most of my colleagues, I refused to wear polyester. Since my recent divorce I had moved from three-piece Brooks Brothers suits to the more rumpled look of corduroy.

I could remember paying attention to the way I sounded even when I was in high school. I had run for president of the student government, and for a crucial speech before the assembled student body I had practiced with a tape recorder for hours to purge my New Jersey accent. Not only did I win that election, but I never said "dese" and "dose" again.

". . . This resistance must be by acts and not mere words, and must be reasonably proportionate to the victim's strength and opportunity. It must be in good faith and without pretense, with an active determination to prevent the violation of the person, and must not be merely passive and perfunctory. . . ."

The defendant wore heavy wing-tipped shoes and tight black socks that went above the calf. As he sat with his legs crossed, I could see the white skin and coarse black hairs on his leg above the sock. At my insistence he was wearing an appropriately serious navy blue suit with a plain white shirt and subdued tie.

". . . However, the fact that a victim finally submits does not necessarily imply that she has consented. Submission to a compelling force, or as a result of being in fear, is not consent. . . ."

The defendant's eyes darted back and forth from one juror to another, searching for evidence of their thoughts. He had a flag of skin like a rooster's leading from his neck to his chin. The tunnel-like nostrils in his upturned nose gave him a strong resemblance to Porky Pig. Can you imagine, I thought to myself, those fat lips pressing close to anyone you loved? Not one of my better-looking defendants. The prosecutor had missed his strongest argument: How, but by rape, could this ugly creature hope to get over with a woman like Lisa Altman? How could a woman so beautiful ever consent to be touched by such a pig?

I responded in my mind to my own argument: Ladies and gentlemen of the jury, as evidence of how depraved and promiscuous this woman is, look at this disgusting and vulgar son of a corporate executive that she chose to degrade and debase herself with. Just look at that face of his. Wouldn't you have run or called for help just on seeing him? But she did neither. She must have wanted him because of some deep psychological problem of self-worth.

". . . It is only required," the judge went on, "that the female resist as much as she possibly can under the circumstances, and the circumstance and conditions surrounding the parties at the time of the alleged offense are to be considered in determining whether adequate resistance was offered. . . ."

"Do you think it'll be all right?" my client whispered.

I nodded.

A short while later three court officers placed their hands on a shared Bible and swore, as the court clerk intoned, "to take the jury to some convenient place and suffer no one to speak to them, nor speak to them yourself."

The court officers led the jury out of the courtroom, and the judge banged his gavel.

Nothing left to do but wait for the verdict, I thought as I stood and headed out of the courtroom.

Chapter 3

A FEW MOMENTS later the elevator doors closed behind me, and I felt the air seep out of me. The heaviness in my arms and shoulders, the effort in my breathing, were unusual this early in the deliberations. The beat of my pulse pounding in my left ear usually came after the verdict, when the tension of waiting was over.

I grabbed my arm and began to rub it. It was more of an itch than a pain, more like tiny needles pricking my skin. I realized I was rubbing the spot that my client had touched after I had completed my cross-examination of the woman. I couldn't bear the sight of my client. Ever since Jenny had left me, I had become increasingly critical of my work, increasingly unhappy about how I was using my skills and energies. This case was not making me feel any better about myself.

I had applied to law school convinced that I could

satisfy some noble expectations as a lawyer. Although I had never articulated what those expectations were, I knew I cared about the poor and the defenseless; I might have had only a hazy sense of what justice was, but I had a deeply felt, intuitive sense of injustice. I hadn't talked out loud about such things, because I hadn't wanted to sound self-righteous or naive, but that outrage over injustice had never anticipated the prospect of representing monsters—which was what I now considered most of my clients to be.

The excitement with which I had begun my career as a criminal defense lawyer—convinced as I was that idealism and ambition were not incompatible— rather quickly dissipated with the realization that the practice of law was a business like any other. I had been nervous about whether I could get clients, but they came. Within a year I was working seventy hours a week and earning a good living. And that workload had continued in the years that followed.

I always felt exhausted after a trial, and that was particularly true now. But it would be months before I would fully realize how different this case was from any other in my career—and the effect it would have on my life.

For most of my years of trying cases, an acquittal would invariably make my spirits soar. Now, in the twenty-second year of my practice, I doubted if I were still capable of that kind of hit. Instead, coming down from the tension and excitement of a trial simply left me feeling depressed. I had never understood the source of that depression. Maybe it was somehow similar to postpartum blues. But wherever it came from, it was real, and with the end of this trial approaching, the depression was already palpable.

Hundreds, I had represented hundreds—trying to keep them out of jail, keep them on the streets. I could no longer deflect the realization—this chilling glimpse of myself—that I had used all my skill and energy on behalf of a collection of criminals. William Betz was rich and had paid me $70,000 to prevent the state from proving he was guilty of rape beyond a reasonable doubt. But who knows? Maybe Betz was innocent.

Most of my clients were poor and probably paid me all the money they had or could steal. Some of my cases were assigned by the Legal Aid Office. The Supreme Court had decided a while ago that everyone, even an indigent, was entitled to a lawyer in a criminal case. As a result, some portion of impoverished clients were assigned by the public defender to private attorneys, who were paid on an hourly basis by the state. About a quarter of my cases came to me this way. These cases didn't pay nearly as well as the work with private clients, but if you handled a number of them at the same time, the money would add up.

The clients assigned by the public defender were the poorest in every respect. Sure, some of the poor ones might have been guilty of crimes brought on by poverty, but their victims hadn't caused their poverty, and most of the victims were equally poor. And most of those equally poor victims didn't go out and mug or rape or kill.

The elevator began to descend. Jenny had waited with me during my first few trials. We would pace the corridors together, chain-smoking, chatting and laughing nervously about details of our life. After those early trials but before Molly was born, Jenny had made a point of being close to the phone at her office. I'd call her several times while I waited for a verdict, and call her again immediately on hearing the news.

It was touching, I thought now, how desperately Jenny had wanted to believe in the innocence of my clients. She, understandably, had become less involved with my work around the same time she had become pregnant and stopped working. After Molly was born, Jenny was too occupied to focus much on who I was taking on as clients. Believing my clients were innocent victims had at one time also been important to me. It must have been.

The elevator stopped to let off and take on passengers. Waiting for a verdict. Waiting for a case to start. For a jury to be picked. A witness to arrive. I waited badly. Such a waste of time. I was incapable of accomplishing anything during these intervals. Certainly not work. Though I sure as hell had work. This case had taken a lot more time than I had expected.

I leaned against the gray metal wall of the elevator. Sometimes it felt as if I had always been waiting. Waiting to get out of law school, waiting to get married, build a law practice, have a child, get a divorce, and still I was waiting: this time to find a point to my life. At least the jury's verdict would be back before then.

"What do you look so upset about, Michael? Did the judge sentence you instead of your client?"

I hadn't noticed the man standing next to me in the

crowded elevator. It was Norman Dogbein. "Hi, Norman. How you feeling?" I asked.

Norman, in his late fifties, had had a heart attack a couple of years ago in the middle of a summation, but that hadn't kept him from taking a lying prosecutor into the corridor a few weeks ago and decking him with a good right. I always admired people who could express their grievances.

"I'm fine, Michael. Fine," he said, and turned to a little black kid about five years old standing in front of us. The boy, who had plaintive dark eyes, was sandwiched between his mother and a cop. "Hey, sonny," Norman said.

The kid looked up at Norman.

"What's the rap, sonny?" Norman asked, smiling playfully and motioning with his head to the man in uniform next to him. "The fuzz pinch you for running numbers?"

The kid smiled back at Norman, but at the same time pressed closer to his mother.

The cop didn't seem to find the question amusing.

Norman turned back to me. "I hear you're on your feet up in Bennett's court. How's it going?" When Norman spoke, he'd lean his large head toward you.

The elevator doors opened. "Buy you a cup of coffee?" I asked.

Norman nodded. We walked toward the cafeteria.

"I guess I should feel good about it. The jury just got the case," I said.

"Bennett's a mean bastard."

"Not so bad. I've known him for years." I held the cafeteria door for Norman. "Jesus, I'm exhausted."

"You get along with those WASP cocksuckers," Norman said.

"Get along with them? I wouldn't say that. One of them just divorced me."

"I'm not surprised. Who could live with you?"

"I can't imagine," I said, and it occurred to me that Bennett wasn't a WASP; he was an Irish Catholic. Obviously, Norman didn't make fine distinctions between "goyim."

The cafeteria was like a large renovated airplane hangar. The walls must have originally been painted yellow, but now seemed closer to brown. Vertical blinds kept the fluorescent light from escaping out the long, narrow windows. The smell of ammonia hung in the air—the linoleum floors must have already received their afternoon mopping.

I led Norman through the turnstile, past the steaming wells of the serving counter. From the stainless-steel urn, I poured coffee into two plastic foam cups. "Here. Sip it, Norman. It'll make us humble."

"Fat chance," Norman said.

"Hey, Mr. Roehmer, I thought you were terrific today." One of the old spectators who frequently attended my trials startled me from behind.

"Thank you," I said. "It's good to see you."

"You really nailed the broad yesterday. I mean you really banged her," he said, and gave me a dirty wink.

"It went all right. Take care of yourself," I said, and started to walk away. I liked the *idea* of fans more than their compliments.

"I bet the jury'll be back in less than an hour." The man pushed back the large horn-rimmed glasses that had slipped down to the bulb of his nose.

"We'll see." I walked away. I hoped he was right about the time it would take for an acquittal—and that it would be an acquittal.

I made my way to the corner of the room, trying not to squeeze the cup too hard. I sat with Norman for about a half hour and listened to his "war stories." I'd heard them a number of times before. Norman, it seemed, had endless energy with which to retell his triumphs. We had shared a number of coffees over the years.

At one point Allen Swid, a reporter who covered the courts for a local paper, approached the table. Plump and balding, he walked as if he were carrying a bucket of water on his head. I nodded to Allen.

"Gentlemen," Swid said. "Anything doing?"

"We're doing waiting," I said.

"Yes, I know. I left before the charge. Had to make a call. Standard charge?"

"Standard charge," I said.

"Any mistakes? Anything you're angry about, Michael?"

"Bennett is too careful to make mistakes."

"The state would have had a much better shot in your case if they'd had a confession," Swid said.

"We don't call them confessions anymore, Allen," Norman said. "We call them involuntary statements. 'Confessions' is too depressing a phrase for defense lawyers."

Allen Swid glanced at Norman and flashed a quick smile, but his interest was in my case, and he kept his attention on me. "You got to admit you were pretty brutal with the woman," Swid said.

"We do the best we can," I said. I had more than once seen casual comments of mine turn up in Swid's articles. I wasn't about to give him anything quotable.

"And a woman who overcame polio, no less," Swid said. At ten, Lisa had apparently beaten the disease by sheer determination. Fortunately I had been able to keep away from the jury as irrelevant information any reference to her heroic struggle with the disease, and the ignorance of her impoverished parents in not having gotten her vaccinated.

"You were really more vicious than I'd ever seen you before. You think that's true?"

"And what the hell do you think a good lawyer like Michael uses a courtroom for, anyway?" Norman asked.

"What do you mean?" Swid asked.

"I mean, a courtroom's where a lawyer's supposed to act out all his emotions. Cathartic, therapeutic. And I'll tell you one thing: it's better than going home and beating your wife."

I looked at Norman and wondered how much he was joking.

"But, after all, Michael, this was a simple case, only one eyewitness—the alleged victim." Swid was baiting me. "A cyclops—isn't that what you call these one-eyewitness cases?"

"She's a most beautiful and appealing witness, and she knows how to look sympathetic. Very hard to deal with," I said.

"Seriously," Swid went on, "don't you think it was peculiar that not one person from her ballet company came to the trial? I was looking to do an interview, but there wasn't one person, not a dancer, no one."

"I noticed," I said. "But some of her fans were there. I overheard some of them talking."

"Weren't you surprised? I mean, for one of the world's most famous dancers? Don't you think that's a little odd?"

"No. She's a loner. She doesn't have anything to do with the people she works with. That's not so odd," I said.

"You sure are good at arguing either side, aren't you, Michael," Swid said.

I smiled, realizing that it was preposterous for me to appear to be defending the victim. "That's what makes me a professional," I said.

"I guess you're not going to give me any pearls today, huh, Michael?" Swid said.

"Like pearls before Swid?" Norman asked.

"I got to pick up some galleys of my story on your case," Swid said, ignoring Norman. "I'm curious if this new editor has left anything that resembles my piece. It's called 'Anatomy of a Celebrity on Trial.'"

"Very catchy," I said.

Allen Swid moved on.

I looked over to Norman. "The penetrating light of the Fourth Estate," I said.

"I wonder if he has any idea how many people think he's an ass," Norman said.

"Oh, to see ourselves as others see us," I said.

"Right," Norman said.

"That's what we lawyers are supposed to be good at so that we can convince jurors of the rightness of our cause," I said.

"Right," Norman said, and began telling me about a trial he had had a few years ago. I'd heard the story several times before.

Eventually Norman finished his story, apologized for having to go, and finally left me in peace.

A few minutes later, Cheryl Hazelton approached me with a cup of coffee. "Mind if I interrupt you?" she asked. Cheryl was a tall black woman, an assistant prosecutor. The prosecutor's office had no more beautiful woman working for it.

"Please join me," I said, although I would have preferred to be alone and quiet for a little while longer.

Cheryl and I had known each other for years. We had tried several cases against each other. A criminal trial could resemble a war experience, and although a defense lawyer did battle against a prosecutor, such shared experiences sometimes created special bonds like the bonds between "war buddies" . . . and that was the relationship between Cheryl and me. I knew Cheryl liked me for not being smug about a drug case I had won against her when she was just starting out in the prosecutor's office.

"You look tired," she said as she took the seat across from me where Norman had been sitting a few moments ago.

"I'm getting too old for this," I said.

"Are you ready to start another case?" she asked.

"What other case?"

"The Larsen case," she said.

I had not quite forgotten about a client of mine who had been waiting in jail for six months at this point, but I certainly hadn't thought of him since the start of my trial with Betz two weeks ago. Larsen was accused of attempting to murder his gay lover.

"We should get going with it soon or else I'm going to get trapped into starting something else," I said. "Taylor probably wants to move it off his calendar, don't you think?"

"Taylor? Taylor's a nutcase, I mean a real hypochondriac," Cheryl said. "In the last case I tried with Taylor, I wanted an adjournment, so I went to speak to him at sidebar. He was sitting there with his pills next to his water pitcher. I asked for an adjournment. Taylor said no. So I coughed. He said two weeks."

"Eccentric, perhaps, but something less than insane," I said. Most people who worked at the courthouse knew that Taylor was a hypochondriac.

"A nutcase," Cheryl said.

"I'd rather deal with him than with Fazio." Cheryl had been the prosecutor in the case I had just finished with Fazio.

Cheryl and I looked over to a nearby table where Judge Fazio was sitting with several other judges. Fazio was smiling, giving no indication that he understood a word anyone was saying. In his midfifties with gray hair, a prominent forehead, deep-set eyes, a rather generous nose, and a jutting, Jeffersonian chin, Anthony Fazio looked like a judge. A year earlier he had been chastised by the chief justice of the state supreme court for having allowed a photograph of himself in judicial robes to be used in promotional materials of a garment company that sold judicial robes. The chief justice had felt it unseemly that the image of one of "his" judges be used for commercial purposes. Judge Fazio probably would have gotten into more trouble if he had been paid for the use of his picture. Apparently Fazio had posed only for the attention he would receive.

"I never realized he was so hard-of-hearing till this last case," Cheryl said, turning back to face me. She was referring to the trial she and I had finished before Fazio about a month ago. I would have wanted to work out a plea bargain with Cheryl in that case because of all the witnesses against my client. In a plea bargain, a defendant agrees to give up his right to a trial and to plead guilty to a less serious offense than the one he is charged with. Prosecutors agree to a plea bargain because the state saves the expense of a trial and avoids the risk of losing the trial; defendants agree to it because they avoid being found guilty of more serious offenses and doing longer time in prison. In the case Cheryl was referring to, she had offered me no real "bargain" of a plea. So we went to trial, and, not surprisingly, I lost.

"You got to admit he looks like a judge," I said.

"I always thought he just wasn't interested in what I was saying."

"Maybe nowadays justice is supposed to be deaf as well as blind," I said.

"Well, nobody's perfect," Cheryl said. "What's the chances of a plea with Larsen?"

"Can you let him out for the time he's served waiting for this trial?" I asked.

"Come on, Michael, you know I can't. Christ, it's attempted murder. Your guy puts a twelve-inch knife

into the guy's stomach. How can I give him a walk?"
A "walk" is a plea bargain by which the defendant
winds up with a non–prison sentence that allows him
to walk out of the courtroom with his lawyer at the
end of the case.

"If you were having trouble getting your witness,
maybe you could justify it."

"No problem," Cheryl said, but we both knew
there was a problem. The corroborating witness had
"gone south" on her. But neither of us would ac-
knowledge that we knew it at this stage in the plea
negotiations.

I nodded and took a sip of coffee. "It was just a
lovers' quarrel," I said.

"Except your guy wasn't scratched, and he weighs
about a hundred pounds more than the victim."

I hated the prospect of having Taylor watch me try
this case and see me humiliate a man who had already
been through hell. "I'm going to have to crucify the
victim. It's demeaning," I said. The way I was feeling
at the moment, "demeaning" was probably an un-
derstatement.

"Right. So why don't we work out a plea?"

"I can't. My guy won't go for anything."

"Right," Cheryl said.

"Taylor should be just as embarrassed as I am. He's
going to have to just sit there and watch me cut that
poor bastard up worse than what my client did to
him."

"Right."

"Some business," I said.

"Right. Some business," Cheryl said.

Cheryl and I walked out of the cafeteria together.

We assured each other that we would get back in touch shortly about the Larson case. I had no idea then that it would take more than three months and that my client would be waiting in jail all that time.

I headed back to wait for the verdict, opened the door of the courtroom, and saw Betz still sitting at his place at counsel table. I decided to wait alone on a bench in the corridor outside.

I would have been very surprised if the jury had not returned an acquittal. If I won, I would have proof that I, and I alone, as defense counsel, had destroyed Lisa in a way that no one else could have. At least, I believed that, and certainly no one could prove otherwise. After all, I had gotten her to admit that she had been aroused by my client. No one else could have gotten her to say that. Probably.

I felt a growing guilt about what I had done to Lisa. Not that I'd had any choice: for me to win, she had to be destroyed. But I was having an odd reaction that reminded me of the only time I'd gone hunting, more than twenty years ago. I'd shot a deer, a lovely, defenseless deer that had frozen in his tracks. When the deer went down, I was overwhelmed with guilt. I had wished immediately, even before the sound of the gunshot had left the forest, that I could have taken back the shot, unpulled the trigger. I had soothed my conscience by telling myself that I hadn't known what I was doing. I hadn't experienced that kind of guilt before or since then—not until this trial. My attack on Lisa had generated the same feelings I'd had as when I'd shot the deer. But this time I'd known exactly what I was doing, and I hadn't yet figured out how I'd soothe my conscience. But I was sure I'd find a way.

A court officer came out of the courtroom to tell me that I was needed inside. The jury had reached a verdict.

Chapter 4

TEN CHILDREN, ALL around the age of four, were playing in the large living room of my house. I owned a substantial family house surrounded by a well-groomed lawn in a lovely suburb of New York. Children's music and snippets of their laughter filled the room and fresh, scented air came from the garden through the large French doors.

Twelve parents were watching. The verdict was only a few hours old, but I was able to be totally involved in a new setting. I was observing the scene through the lens of a video camera balanced on my shoulder. I was focused exclusively on my lovely daughter, Molly, who was lying facedown on the rug.

Jenny, my ex-wife, was standing next to me. We had lived in this house for eleven years, until we separated and she got an apartment in the center of town. Jenny and several of the other mothers were singing "The Bunnies Are Sleeping":

See the little bunnies sleeping till it's nearly noon.
Come and let us gently wake them with a merry
tune. Oh how still. Are they ill? Hop little bunnies!
Hop! Hop! Hop!

All the children jumped up from the rug and began
hopping. I finally aimed the video camera at some of
the other children. I then quickly panned the adults in
the room before returning my attention to Molly.

Everyone clapped and laughed at the happy, hopping children.

"Charming," Charles Donner said. Charles had
been a friend of mine since we'd begun law school
together twenty-five years ago.

"Aren't they darling!" Charles's wife, Eleanor,
said.

Molly ran over to me. I put down the camera and
she gave me a big hug. I kissed her.

"Are you having a good time, sweetheart?" I
asked.

"Yes, Daddy. I'm really, really glad you could
come," Molly said.

"So am I," I said.

"Daddy?"

"Yes?"

"Daddy, did you bring home the bacon?"

I laughed. Molly and I had a little ritual. When I
went off to trial, Molly would ask me where I was
going, and I would say I was going to bring home the
bacon. "Yes, sweetheart. I brought home the bacon,"
I said.

"Good. Daddy, can I come with you next time you
go to court and watch you win your case?"

"Isn't it a fact, young lady," I said in a stentorian, self-mocking voice, "that I've told you on numerous occasions that I don't *always* win my cases?"

Molly smiled, enjoying the exchange. "Yes. But you *usually* win, don't you, Daddy?"

"But I put it to you, Ms. Witness," I continued in the same self-mocking voice for the benefit of Molly rather than the adults standing by, "isn't it a tissue of lies to imply an 'always' when the undeniable truth is merely 'usually'?"

Molly giggled. "Tissues aren't for lies. They're for sneezing, Daddy. Bye-bye," she said, and ran off to join her friends.

"You still have the bacon ritual, I see," Jenny said.

"As you know, I'm very big on rituals," I said.

"Only too well, sweetheart," Jenny said.

"Give me the camera, Michael," Eleanor said, "so I can take a picture of our conquering hero."

"Sorry, Eleanor, I'm the director, not the talent."

"Well, you're certainly the talent in the courtroom," Eleanor said.

"Yes, I'm certain we're all impressed with your skill," Jenny said with less than total conviction.

"Michael, do we all get copies of your video masterpiece?" Pebble asked.

"Sure," I said. "I can also give you a deal on forty hours of 'Molly: The Early Years.'"

"Just the parts that include our son would be fine, thank you," Pebble said.

"You think Michael is joking," Jenny said. "The first tape begins with him holding Molly in his arms when she was six days old."

"I set the camera up on a tripod," I said. "And I

said, 'This is my daughter, and this is the start of a primary document that she can take to her shrink when she gets old enough, so that, unlike me, she doesn't have to rely on dreams or chase distorted memories.'"

Everyone laughed.

Jenny shook her head. "He also wanted to present his version of what really happened," she said.

Everyone laughed again.

"You wanted to give yourself the best defense, no doubt," Charles said.

"Exactly," I said.

Everyone laughed.

"I don't know why you haven't shown it to *your* shrink yet," Jenny said.

"I should. Maybe he'll think I'm not such a monster after all," I said.

"I guess we should gather up the heirs and get going. It's getting dark," Pebble said.

"Thank you all for coming," I said.

I assumed no one wanted to leave, because no one made a move to get their coats.

"Well, thank you. And congratulations again. It was a sensational win, Killer," Eleanor said.

"God knows, on some level I must still love winning," I said. "Or why else would I keep trying so hard?"

"I've been meaning to ask you," Stan said. "Do you feel any responsibility for what your clients do after you get them back out on the street?" Stan was a surgeon; he and his wife, Pebble, were my next-door neighbors. I never liked him much, but he had a sweet daughter who was Molly's best friend.

"As a doctor, would you feel responsible for what a murderer does after you repaired his trigger finger?" I said.

"The system can't function without advocates, adversaries fighting it out," Charles said.

"Charles, that's what you and I learned in law school. But the system can function with other advocates. It doesn't need me," I said.

"The problem is that you're too good at it. You're not just an equal adversary—you're a killer, Killer," Eleanor said.

"That's kind of you to say, Eleanor," I said.

"My wife means 'killer,' of course, in the best sense, Michael," Charles said with a smile.

"Well, that's what I'm trained for. Who knows—I might have been defending an innocent man," I said.

"This is the only kind of case that really upsets me," Jenny said.

"That beheading case—that didn't bother you?" Eleanor asked.

"That was awful, but somehow, rape . . ." Jenny's voice trailed off.

"Every time you win an exciting case, Eleanor asks me if I set up any thrilling trusts lately," Charles said. "By the way, how's Bear doing?" Charles was referring to Judge Singer, the judge I had clerked for.

"Not well, I'm afraid," I said. "I'm going to miss him." The judge had retired three years ago, after twenty-five years on the bench. For the last two weeks he had been a few blocks from the courthouse, at St. John's Hospital, dying. He was dying because his liver had sentenced him to death.

"He's a tough old bastard. Maybe he'll pull through," Charles said.

"He's been very good to me, Charles, over the years, whenever I needed advice," I said. Bear could be a mean son of a bitch who would scream at lawyers in his court if they were unprepared. He had a temper, but his anger came out because he really cared. And he certainly never acted in anger toward me.

"I always envied your relationship with him," Charles said.

"Stick around for a little while. I just want to get one of those," I said, pointing to Charles's drink.

I walked over to the maid and picked up a drink from her tray.

"Thank you for inviting us," a woman I had never met before said. "I hope that our daughters can become good friends."

"I'm glad you could come," I said politely.

"We saw that Altman woman in *Giselle*," the man next to the woman said.

"Oh, really?" I said.

"She was very attractive and very convincing in that," the woman said.

"I must say, she got better reviews in *Giselle* than at her trial," the man said.

"You must say?" I said, and tried to smile. "You people have no idea what it's like being beaten up in a cross-examination," I said.

"The newspapers this time were brutal," the man said, and laughed.

"Critics are so fucking fickle, I must say. Excuse me," I said, smiling, but with anger in my voice.

I walked away from the couple, leaving them taken aback by my language. I was probably as surprised as they were by my anger. I couldn't remember the last time I had talked like that to strangers, particularly strangers who were just trying to be flattering.

I knew that I had told Charles I was going to come back to him once I had gotten a drink, but I really didn't want to talk anymore to anyone about anything.

I went over to the terrace doors, opened them, and stepped out onto the brick terrace. Alone in the gathering night, I walked to the edge of the terrace. A dozen cars were parked in the circular driveway leading up to the front door.

I looked back into the house and watched the animated party for a moment. The music, talk, and children's laughter continued. Jenny could be seen through the window, engaged in intense conversation.

The cold night air awakened me. I thought about what Stan had asked me, or at least what was implied by his question. I wondered how many times I had been asked what I got out of being a criminal lawyer. I hated most of my clients. I spent much of my time in depressing places like prisons. The money wasn't great. As a criminal lawyer I was looked down on by judges, other lawyers, the public—except perhaps the couple to whom I had just been so rude, and Eleanor, who was bored with her husband.

It wasn't hard to explain why very few lawyers did criminal work and even fewer went on doing it for any length of time. I didn't have a good explanation for why I had remained in this work for so long.

I could see Jenny through the windows of the French doors leading out to the terrace. She was pointing a finger at Charles, making a point. I loved her earnestness. I always had.

I could have killed her when she told me she was going to leave me. She had worked for years before Molly was born, and I was sure that she could have gone back to work without breaking up the marriage. Her work was just an excuse to get out of the marriage. We'd had so many problems that had gone unresolved for so long, the distance between us obviously seemed unbridgeable to her. I had understood that—I understood that, but I wanted to kill her anyway. No, "kill" is too strong. I had been furious. I was still angry.

Her agreement to leave Molly with me, even though she retained equal custody, must have been painful. I knew that she had agonized over it. She loved Molly as much as I did, and I knew she believed me when I assured her that as soon as she was ready to take Molly, we would begin having her divide her time between our respective houses. In the meantime Molly stayed with her mother on weekends at her apartment ten minutes away. Weren't we the model, modern couple!

I wondered how much of my anger was over losing Jenny and how much was over losing control of the relationship. Whatever the mixed sources of my anger, I still managed to conduct myself in a civilized manner. I had used my genuine concern for Molly to restrain my rage. I'm sure I wouldn't have been as controlled if I hadn't had the welfare of my child to focus on.

The irony was that Jenny and I rarely had fights over anything that really bothered us personally. Here was I, a professional fighter, and over the years I had often expressed rage, or indignation, or joy, or sadness—but I only seemed capable of doing that in a courtroom.

For years I had been troubled by my difficulty in expressing in my personal life the same range and depth of feeling. My relationship with Jenny had often seemed infinitely more threatening than a packed courtroom. Frequently, the problem had not just been in the expression of feeling but in a failure to experience those feelings at all—or, as Jenny had often claimed, to experience them with sufficient intensity to recognize them.

Getting angry in a personal confrontation could mean actually losing control and becoming vulnerable, and that could be terrifying. Ironically, I showed virtuoso skill in the courtroom at *appearing* transported by emotion, when in reality my emotions were on a tether every moment.

All the emotions skillfully displayed in a courtroom had a purpose—winning. I wondered if I was guilty of overkill in the way that I had disposed of Lisa, and if I had gone at her with more than I had needed.

I turned away from the house, looked down the long driveway, took a pull on my drink. The darkness down the driveway seemed thicker because of the lights of the house behind me. The air was moist and warm for November. The dusk spread like a mist to the edge of the property, where a streetlamp threw some light. The large ironwork gate framed a spray of gray light behind it. As I stared at the gate, I noticed what could have been a figure of someone standing just behind it. The black shadow didn't move, but as I looked more closely, I saw it could have been the outline of a person. The distance and the darkness made it impossible to determine if it was a man or a woman, but it did seem to be a human silhouette.

Suddenly the headlights of a rapidly moving car appeared on the road outside the house. The car passed the front gate, casting its light on the silhouette. For a fleeting moment the shape became clear. There was no question there was a person there, and it was a woman. I had a moment's panic as I realized that the form looked very much like Lisa Altman.

"What the hell would she be doing there?" I muttered to myself. When the car passed, the image returned to a silhouette, a kind of menacing, grayish ghost. I took a few tentative steps toward the figure, then stopped. I didn't want to confront it. I turned and went back into the house to rejoin my daughter's party.

As I stepped into the living room, Jenny walked toward me. She was a handsome woman, tall and straight, with an honest, open face. Her new short haircut, worn boyishly with a part, emphasized her no-nonsense appearance. Of course, she still wore no makeup.

"I should have thought to look for you on the terrace," Jenny said. The flecks of orange in her dark brown eyes always gave a warmth to her gaze, and the little crow's-feet in the corner of her eyes lent even more warmth to her smile.

"Hi, Jen," I said. I put my arm around her and hugged her affectionately. She didn't respond to my embrace.

"So how's single life treating you?" I asked. We had been divorced for six months, but it had been almost a year since she had moved out.

"Oh, Michael, it's a jungle out there." Her sarcasm was new, and I didn't find it very attractive.

"I don't know why you ever married me in the first place," I said.

"Because you overpowered me the way you overpower juries. That's why."

"Maybe we can still sort things out."

"You don't give up, do you."

"You know I hate to lose."

"You haven't lost. There was no winner or loser."

"Oh, really? You're sure about that?" I asked.

"*You* made our marriage into a contest."

"The divorce was uncontested," I said, making a technical and irrelevant point.

"We're both better off now, and Molly will also be better off in the long run."

"We all live in the short run."

"I won't argue with you, sweetheart. You make a living out of arguing."

"I know. I'm good at it."

"You'll find a woman who'll like living with 'the killer in the courtroom.' That's all you ever wanted to be."

"I wish you didn't have such contempt for what I do."

"You have as much contempt for it as I do," she said.

"We weren't like that in the beginning," I said. We had met when Jenny was fresh out of Vassar, still very much the innocent product of her WASP upbringing. The idyllic country life she'd had as a kid in northwest Connecticut had always seemed a different world from the Newark that I had known. Since her parents had treated her as if she'd died when she married me, I never did get to learn much about that life firsthand.

"You were different then," she said.

"We both were," I said.

"I know. It's nobody's fault. I just couldn't deal with your obsession with your work," she said. "And the way it infected our relationship."

"This sounds like a subject you've discussed with your shrink."

"I have to admit it did come up," Jenny said.

"Isn't it a fact that I'm dealing with a prepared witness?" I asked, half jokingly.

"When I married you, I thought you really cared about people."

"I still do care about people—*certain* people: Molly and, believe it or not, you," I said.

Jenny looked around the room. "It's a very nice party. Molly seems really happy," she said.

"Judith is doing a terrific job. She's the best nanny in the world. Molly hardly misses you."

"You are a bastard. I see her as much as you do."

"A bastard?" I smiled and tried to put my arm around her again.

Jenny shrugged my arm off her shoulder. "All you hot shot criminal lawyers are so terribly perceptive about other people, predicting how we'll respond to your shrewd tactics, manipulating us."

"Jenny . . ."

"But in your personal lives, with your enormous egos, you have no understanding of your own behavior. For all the time we lived together you even claimed to have no *interest* in it."

This wasn't the first time I'd heard this indictment, and it was clear to me that Jenny was right. It was also clear to me that her latest attack was a response to my reference to her abandoning Molly. I knew very well that Jenny had an open nerve of guilt over that. I was sorry I had attacked her. It was only a reflex.

"Calm down, Jenny. Please. The truth is I miss you," I said.

Chapter 5

I WALKED UP to the front door of a large hospital building and entered. It was the morning after I had won my case, and I was on my way to visit my sick friend and mentor, Lloyd Singer.

I made my way to an elevator, got on, ascended, got off on the sixth floor, and walked over to the nurses' station.

"Good morning, Mr. Roehmer," the nurse said. "You're late this morning."

"My trial is over. How is he today?" I asked.

"Basically the same. I don't think it will be much longer. I'm sorry, Mr. Roehmer. Although he did seem to come awake for a few moments after you left yesterday."

I nodded and headed down the corridor.

I entered the mint green room of my friend and sat down beside him. Bear's bony body was a yellow-brown from the breakdown of his liver. He was breathing in quick, short breaths, unaware of my arrival.

"Good morning, Bear," I said. He didn't move.

I sat quietly for a few moments, then reached over and took Bear's hand and held it. I shared the silence for a few more moments with my friend. He was asleep, maybe even in a coma.

During these last three years Bear had often complained to me about his liver. "My goddamn liver," he would say.

"The 'problem' with his liver," Jenny said to me more than once, "is that it's pickled in Jameson Irish Whiskey." I, of course, never dared to mention that to Bear, for fear of hurting his feelings. I always thought that, in a weird way, Jenny was jealous of my relationship with Bear.

I viewed most judges as adversaries, if not enemies. Judges often came from the upper classes, representing power and rules that the poor and uneducated never understood. Ever since my clerkship with him I'd always considered Bear to be different from any other judge, although he was the wealthy son and grandson of lawyers. He was always generous and kind to me.

I always admired the way Bear had retained his strong belief in our system of justice. I might have started out with lofty notions about "the law," but I had sure as hell lost them a long time ago.

It had been painful for me these last few years to watch my friend, this once powerful chunk of a man, slowly dying. In contrast to the musty smell of tradition and power in Bear's chambers, the antiseptic odor of the hospital room unnerved me.

"Well, I won the case. You would have been very proud," I said, stroking my friend's hand. He still lay unmoving, his eyes closed. "I picked a good jury, but the key was the victim . . . or the alleged victim . . . who knows. Guilty or innocent, I got her on the cross, no question about that."

I paused for a few moments. I knew that Bear probably wouldn't have been so proud of what I had done to that woman. I wasn't so proud of it either.

"This is a long way from your chambers in the old courthouse. I loved the oak-paneled walls. . . . Even my little office next door to your chambers when I was your clerk had oak-paneled walls. . . . And that's where you swore me in as prosecutor. . . . Whatever happened to your wonderful mahogany desk? I loved the smell of all the books in your chambers." I looked down at Bear's sleeping face and continued talking—I assumed to myself. "You used to joke that it was the smell of tradition and order . . . not like the goddamn smell of this room. I'm sure you hate it here, too."

I turned my friend's hand over in mine, hesitating for a moment. "Bear, I miss our talks. I know you can't hear me, but I need to talk to you."

I looked at the lines on the inside of Bear's hand. "How did you do it? I mean, how did you keep it all together?"

I looked up from his hand to confirm that he was still asleep.

"I'm losing it, Bear. I'm terrified of losing control. I've grown to hate the people I fight for. Monsters. I used to love their worlds. The more desperate they were, the more fascinating I found them. It used to make me feel so alive. Now I feel dead.

"I know it would be wrong to blame everything on my work. Obviously my shrink is right that most of my personality was formed before I decided to become a lawyer. But I'm sure that over the years the problems I brought into adult life have been made a lot worse by my work."

I struggled to find the main source of my complaint At this point I simply didn't know. All I understood was that I was close to breaking. I blathered on to Bear, feeling a certain freedom in the knowledge that he wasn't taking in what I was saying.

"The constant exposure to so many lies has made me incapable of trusting people. I haven't made a new friend in maybe twenty years. I can't meet people without automatically sizing up character and trustworthiness, searching out evil motives. I don't know if you ever noticed, but I have this reflex of recalling all inconsistent statements, no matter how trivial. Good habits for a criminal lawyer—if only they didn't bleed into my personal life . . . as if I have a personal life."

At this point the dialogue with Bear continued in my head. I started to feel I was in the middle of a summation. And I was just warming to a climax. "Destroying witnesses has led to an arrogance, to an inflated sense of control over people that's not so easy to leave behind in the courtroom. The temptation to dominate a social situation or individual . . . sometimes it's irresistible. I'm sure this adversarial reflex helped destroy my marriage. I know how much you liked Jenny.

"Bear, I can't stand the fact that I destroyed that woman. She seemed so vulnerable. Maybe she led my client on. I really never knew. But I do know I hurt her. She didn't have a chance against me. It might have been necessary, but . . . I think I enjoyed it. Yes, I actually enjoyed doing it. I felt excited, thrilled while I did it. I keep thinking about her."

Bear's eyes opened. His lips parted. They were dry. I removed a washcloth from the white nightstand next to the bed and dampened it in the water pitcher on top of the nightstand. I patted Bear's lips with the moist cloth.

Bear struggled to speak. "Michael," he said in a near whisper, "we've seen so many acts of inhumanity in our lives." I could see that each word was a struggle for him.

I clutched my friend's hand again. "That's true, Bear."

"You know I've always been sustained by my belief in God," Bear said.

"Yes, I know."

Bear struggled to keep his eyes opened. "There was one thing I wanted to hear from you, Michael."

"Yes, Bear?"

"Tell me the truth, Michael. How do you think I'll be judged in heaven?"

"I'm sure you'll be judged fairly, Bear." I stroked the back of my friend's hand.

Bear closed his eyes. A moment later he reopened them. It was obvious that my friend was frightened.

"Michael, you must help me," Bear pleaded.

"Of course, Bear," I said.

Bear tried to lift his head up from the pillow to look into my eyes. "You must help me, Michael."

"How can I help you, Bear?"

"Help me, Michael. No one can represent a client better than you. You're the best. You must defend me. You must speak on my behalf. You're the only one I would trust. Will you do that for me, Michael?"

"Bear, I can't do that. You know I can't do that."

Bear closed his eyes again. A moment later he reopened them. This time there was an angry look on his face. "Tell me one thing, Michael."

"Yes, Bear."

"Did I send enough of those bastards away?" Bear began to laugh, a dry, high-pitched, shrill laugh.

"You did the best you could, Bear." I forced myself to smile.

Chapter 6

IT WAS THE following day and I was sitting next to Norman Dogbein and a few other defense lawyers in front of the wooden rail separating the well of the courtroom from the mostly empty rows of spectator seats behind me. Judge Fazio was on the bench, and the usual assortment of attendants were present: court officers, clerk, stenographer, prosecutor.

Over all the years I had been in court, the grimmest times for me had been the sentencing days, when mothers, wives, or kids of the defendants would sit like beaten-down, pathetic victims and listen to lawyers use phrases like "a life of poverty," "without the benefit of a father," and "driven to a life of crime."

On a sentencing day, after each lawyer spoke, it would be the defendant's turn. Some would beg; others would defiantly insist they were innocent; most would sullenly stare at the judge and say nothing. When defendants were given their opportunity to influence the judge, the judge would usually send them to prison.

Although the trial could be seen as theater, it was easy to forget that the victim often bled real blood; and that at the end of the performance, when the play was over, the defendant often went off to a terrifying punishment.

As I awaited my turn, my mind drifted to the time when I was just starting out. I used to be terribly nervous on sentencing day as I watched one defendant after another stand up to hear the announcement of his fate. I used to try to imagine what it would be like if I were the one about to learn how I would spend the next five or ten years of my life. I would tremble inside.

It had been a long time since I had trembled inside. I no longer put myself in the skin of these people.

The procession of people being sent away to prison this morning had begun on time. The first defendant on the list had been brought from the jury box to stand next to his lawyer. The lawyer recited the few laudable moments in his client's twenty-five-year life, touching only lightly on the six arrests and three prior convictions for drug-related crimes.

Over the years, as I awaited my turn for my clients, I must have watched more than a thousand defendants being sentenced. While I had always found the process upsetting, this day it all seemed somehow grotesque, more a scene from Goya than from Daumier.

As a prosecutor, I had convicted dozens of criminals, but I had never argued that any of them should be sent to prison; I always left that up to the judge. As a defense lawyer, I had always fought to keep people out of jail. But now, as I sat there in court watching so-called justice being meted out, I saw myself as nothing more than a necessary prop, constitutionally mandated, whose involvement gave more legitimacy to the appearance of justice.

I realized, of course, that something had to be done with vicious criminals while society figured out a better alternative to prisons. I certainly didn't have a clue about what that better alternative was, nor did I have any bright ideas about how to eliminate the causes of crime. But in the meantime, I didn't like seeing myself as a prop, and I couldn't take any comfort, as I used to, in the thought that it wasn't *I* who was sending my clients to prison.

The lawyer standing before the judge was referring to a presentence report. Prepared by the probation department, the reports summarize defendants' lives and contain recommendations to the judge on what to do with offenders. I had already read the one on my client this morning.

I was in court to speak on behalf of Sherry Parruco. She had been convicted six weeks earlier of attempting to murder her boyfriend in a hardware store. A relatively simple case. With an array of witnesses against my client, I would have been eager to work out a plea with the prosecutor, my friend Cheryl Hazelton, but the "bargain" she offered me was no better than what I could have gotten for Sherry if we had lost at trial. So we went to trial and, of course, we lost. Taxpayers paid thousands for a judge, all his attendants, the prosecutor, the detectives, and for me as well, a lawyer assigned to the case through the Legal Aid office. And we came to the same point we would have reached if the trial had been avoided by a plea. Justice was often expensive and time-consuming.

When Sherry was convicted, I experienced the verdict as a decision against me personally and not her. I knew it was irrational, but I always took a conviction personally, as if the jury were rendering an opinion containing some disapproval of me. (Although I was not so irrational as to lose sight of the fact that it was, indeed, the client and not I who went to jail.) Fortunately, I won most of my cases, but my job would have been a lot easier if most of my clients hadn't been guilty. Almost all of them *were* guilty, however, if not of the crime for which they were being charged, then of something else.

Most of the lawyers in the courtroom were familiar to me. As a prosecutor, I had tried cases against some of them, and as a defense lawyer, I had tried cases with some of them as co-counsel when more than one defendant was being tried on the same indictment. Having been through many sentencings, all the lawyers sat stone-faced. All except, perhaps, the lawyer on his feet, whom I hadn't ever seen before. He looked young.

My prosecutor friend Cheryl Hazelton remained seated at her place at counsel table. Cheryl was smartly dressed in a black silk crepe suit, a white-on-white shirt, and a red-and-gray striped tie pulled up loosely around the collar. Her dark black skin glistened against the very white shirt. She certainly knew how to dress. Cheryl had begun her career as a prosecutor in Bear's courtroom and had worked there on and off for years. As she'd increased in experience and confidence, Cheryl had become very effective. She was a good lawyer with a good sense of humor.

The first case I ever tried against Cheryl had been in Bear's courtroom and had involved a great deal of heroin. The arresting officers had not shown up to testify when they were supposed to, and Bear had reluctantly agreed to Cheryl's request to adjourn to the following day. She took the heroin down to her office and left it on her desk for a few minutes. When she returned, the heroin had vanished. And so had her case.

The following morning Bear was beside himself. When he'd finished yelling at her, I, as the defense lawyer, had demanded a dismissal of the case. Bear had had no choice but to accede to my demand.

Judge Fazio asked if the young lawyer before him had any corrections to make on the presentence report on his client. A judge was required to ask every defense lawyer that same question before passing sentence. Fazio had positioned the loudspeakers on his desk even more closely to himself than he had during the trial. I assumed that without a jury present he felt less embarrassed about his poor hearing.

"I'm glad you asked that question, Your Honor," the young lawyer said earnestly. "The record seems to go on at great length about all the arrests and convictions, but there's no mention of the fact that Mr. Russell was the captain of his high school football team and had even been nominated for a citizenship award."

"I can't imagine how our probation department could have missed such crucial details of Mr. Russell's life," the judge said sarcastically.

"Yes, sir. The criminal record alone gives a very incomplete picture of my client. He was also abandoned by his father at a very early age."

Norman and I turned to each other to share looks of restrained astonishment. "This is a new level of incompetence for the probation department. I hope it doesn't tarnish their reputation," Norman whispered to me with a smile.

"Why, thank you for the correction, Counselor," the judge said, and turned to the rest of us sitting in the courtroom. "Gentlemen, this young man's relentless pursuit of the facts on behalf of his client should be an inspiration to all of you."

The young counselor looked over at his client and smiled. His huge black client looked down at the floor in front of him. He was obviously trying to give the appearance of a pathetic victim of circumstance, but I also had the feeling that in the next moment he would be capable of tearing his lawyer's head off.

The judge sentenced the young lawyer's client to the maximum number of years allowed by law. Without saying a word to his lawyer, the prisoner quietly accompanied the court officers out of the courtroom.

"Next," Judge Fazio barked.

"Sherry Parruco," the court clerk called out, reading from a list.

Sherry Parruco, the young, plump woman in the middle of the row of defendants in the jury box, stood up. Like the other defendants in custody awaiting sentence, she was wearing handcuffs. Her hair was a wedge of orange, cut short and reaching straight up. She was escorted by a court officer to her place at counsel table.

I stepped forward with my briefcase.

"Your Honor, I'm sure, is familiar with the facts of this case, and the state will rely on the court's discretion with regard to sentence imposed," Cheryl said.

"The state, I take it, doesn't want to accept any responsibility for the difficult decisions," Judge Fazio said.

"I wouldn't put it quite that way. We place our total confidence in your good hands," Cheryl responded, with a smile bordering on coquettishness.

"I'm flattered," Judge Fazio said sarcastically, and turned to me. "Counselor, did you want to be heard before I pass sentence?"

"Since the trial was so recent, I guess there is no need for me to repeat the evidence," I said.

"That's correct," Judge Fazio snapped.

"The jury heard all the testimony about how Ms. Parruco's boyfriend unmercifully abused and provoked her over the years," I said. "I think it fair to assume by the jury's verdict of guilty that they considered the evidence of provocation a more relevant factor in determining her sentence than in establishing a defense to the charge."

"Do you, Counselor?" Judge Fazio asked with obvious disbelief. "Do you?"

"That's right," I answered defiantly.

"Maybe the jury simply didn't believe your client had any provocation at all," Judge Fazio said, and looked over at the defendant. "Ms. Parruco, would you like to say anything on your own behalf before I pass sentence?"

"Only that the bastard had it coming, sir," Sherry Parruco said, tilting her chin upward at the judge.

"You have been found guilty by a jury of your peers," Judge Fazio said, "of beating your boyfriend over the head with a lead pipe and then trying to set him on fire."

"Judge, can I just say that we all make mistakes," Sherry said, interrupting him.

"Oh really, Ms. Parruco? What would you say yours was?" Judge Fazio asked.

"Mine was in not using enough lighter fluid," Sherry said.

The court reporter laughed as she typed. Others in the courtroom smiled. I looked around the courtroom. Suddenly I noticed Lisa Altman seated near the door in the back row. She was staring at me.

I couldn't imagine what she was doing there. Why was she following me? How did she even know where to find me? I may have a disturbed nut on my hands, I thought. And there was nothing I liked less than having to deal with some irrational hysteric. The best part of being a lawyer was feeling safe and in control in a courtroom. When a case was over, I didn't need its losers menacing me.

An older woman a few rows in front of Lisa stood. "Judge, Sherry is a good girl," the woman said.

"What was that?" Judge Fazio asked.

"A woman in the back of the courtroom is speaking to you," Cheryl said.

"Who is that? Please step forward," Judge Fazio said.

The woman walked forward to the well of the courtroom.

"What is your name, madam?" Judge Fazio asked.

"Arlene—Arlene Parruco, Your Honor. I'm Sherry's mother. I wanted to say something. If Your Honor would be so kind?"

"I'll allow you."

"Your Honor, I . . ." The woman began to cry. "I just wanted to say that Sherry is a good girl. She never gave me any trouble. This wouldn't have happened if that wop hadn't started it. He must have had it coming."

Cheryl struggled to control her laughter.

"I would like to point out to you, madam," Judge Fazio said, "that on my father's side I am also of Italian heritage—northern Italian."

"Then Your Honor should know what I'm talking about," the woman continued, undaunted. "We should be ashamed of some of us. Please don't send my daughter away. This won't ever happen again."

"Thank you, madam. If you have nothing further to say, you may return to your seat," Judge Fazio said.

"Thank you, Your Honor. It was a pleasure, I'm sure," the woman said. She turned, nodded at her daughter, and walked with great dignity back to her seat. Lisa was still watching me from the back of the courtroom.

"Considering the harm inflicted, the need to deter others, as well as the community's right to exact retribution from those who commit such terrible crimes," Judge Fazio said, "I hereby sentence you to state prison for a maximum term allowed by law, in

this case"—the judge looked down at his notes—
"ten years, with a minimum of five years before the
parole commission may consider your release. People
simply have to learn to take responsibility for their
behavior. But even if they don't learn anything, they
should be punished. Thank you."

Sherry turned to me, her lawyer. "What's he out of
his fuckin' mind, Michael? The bastard really did
have it coming."

"I'm sorry, Sherry," I said.

Sherry turned to the judge. "What are you out of
your fucking mind?" she screamed. "The guy was a
bastard."

The court officers approached Sherry and grabbed
her by the elbows.

"I should be thanked, you asshole," Sherry screamed
at the judge. "I would've made the world safer if
I'd destroyed the creep."

The court officers led Sherry away.

"Well, Michael," Judge Fazio said, "I guess we can
all sleep a little easier tonight now that *I've* made the
world a little bit safer."

Like it's really going to make a difference, I thought
to myself as I threw my papers into my briefcase.
Then I remembered Lisa. I turned around to look for
her in the courtroom, but she was gone.

Chapter 7

THE DAY AFTER Sherry was sent away, I went to my mid-town office in the shadow of St. Patrick's Cathedral. I was working behind my large wooden desk. Papers were strewn all over it and law books were opened and piled on top of each other. This was the way my desk usually looked.

My secretary, Sylvia, entered. She was a small, slight woman in her early sixties. She always wore dark dresses down to her narrow ankles. Her long, thin fingers seemed delicate and fragile. But after eighteen years I knew there was nothing delicate or fragile about Sylvia. When she wasn't complaining, she always made it clear to me by the look on her face that she was silently suffering. But she worried about me—about my health, my career, and my marital status. Once, I had gotten into a minor car accident, and she told me afterward that she felt guilty because she hadn't worried about my driving before the accident. Since my parents had died over twenty years ago, Sylvia had become the closest thing I had to a mother—with all the good and bad that that entailed.

"I cleaned out all your old files in your filing cabinet," Sylvia said proudly.

"Oh, really? Why did you do that?" I asked.

"I got rid of folders that you haven't looked at for years." Sylvia often answered my questions indirectly.

"You got rid of my cases? But I didn't want them thrown out."

"I didn't throw them out. I put them in dead storage. They have a bin in the basement here. It's called dead storage."

"That's a relief. At least you didn't throw them out. But I didn't want them in dead storage. I wanted them as they were, all neatly arranged chronologically in my file cabinet."

"It didn't make any sense to keep them all. You never looked at them. Some were twenty years old. If you ever really need one, I can go down to the basement," she said.

"I liked having all my cases together."

"Right. So now you have the last five years together."

"Right," I said.

"I thought you'd be pleased I'm finally getting you a little organized, putting away some of the garbage you never have a reason to look at."

"Those files aren't garbage."

"The files were garbage and the clients were garbage."

"Thank you, Sylvia. I'm sure I'll get used to my empty file cabinets."

"Someone's got to look after you."

"But you're going to make me crazy."

Sylvia smiled. "You're just saying that," she said, and finally left the room.

I walked over to the file cabinet that Sylvia had half-emptied for me. Hundreds of manila folders filled with cases were missing from the four steel drawers. I was upset. Not that I really needed them. Sylvia was right about that: I rarely, if ever, looked at the contents of a file once a case was closed. But what I now found disturbing was the statement made by their physical departure, the realization that once a case was over, it really no longer had anything to do with me—I could just as well not have tried it. Somehow the presence of those old case files in my office had implied they still had some connection to me. "Dead storage" made them sound like they were no longer appropriate to keep around, even as souvenirs.

A logbook of clients was on top of the cabinet. The logbook contained a list of names, and each name had next to it the crime charged, the date I took on the case, a notation of how the client came to me, the status of the case, and the money paid and still owing, if any.

About a quarter of my clients were assigned to me by the public defender; the rest were sent to me from other lawyers or previous clients, or they were the previous clients themselves who had been charged with something new after I had gotten them off of an earlier charge.

As I flipped through the pages of the logbook, I thought about the clients I had worked so hard for over the years. What a motley array of miscreants! The full assortment of serious felonies. The horrors that people were capable of committing!

I threw the client logbook back on top of the cabinet and opened the drawer to see which files remained. I didn't realize until later that I was thinking about my cases because I wanted to see in what way the Lisa Altman case might be different from the others. Rape was such a terrible crime, regardless of how much or how little force was used. I had tried other rape cases in the past, but they hadn't affected me any differently than any of the other terrible crimes and criminals I had defended.

I had thought of Lisa often since the trial. Then, she had appeared at my house on the night of Molly's party. And just now, a few hours ago, she had showed up again, at Sherry's sentencing. I removed Lisa's large file from the cabinet, brought it over to my desk, laid it on top of the open law books, and removed the folder with newspaper clippings of Lisa's performances. Another folder held a batch of photographs of Lisa dancing, and I pulled them out. One of the photographs had caught her in a leap, her legs spread wide apart, her arms outstretched as if she were flying. She looked as if she could have *flown* away from someone threatening her.

I didn't like the fact that Lisa knew where I lived, that she had come lurking around when my daughter was home, though I didn't think Molly was in any real danger. There was nothing in Lisa's history or in what I sensed of her from the trial that made me think she'd try anything with Molly. I didn't know if Lisa was trying to spook me or was trying to learn something about me. What I did know for sure was that I didn't want her being around my house.

No matter how well you thought you knew people, they were always capable of surprising you, particularly if they thought they had a grievance—and she probably did think that. And Lisa probably did have a grievance. I had treated her mercilessly on the witness stand. I did what I had to do, but that was probably little comfort to Lisa—and it was little comfort to me, either, at this point.

I pulled open the bottom drawer of my desk and took out the bottle of brandy I always kept there. I removed a glass from my top drawer and poured myself a drink. If I'd heeded my father's wishes and become a surgeon, at least I wouldn't have had people skulking around my house.

Sylvia hadn't been wrong to get rid of the old files. The clients who walked through the door of my office were unconnected, without pattern or logic. There was no progression in the sequence of the cases, none leading inevitably to another. It simply didn't make any difference where the old files were buried. The clients seemed a random collection of characters, events, war stories, funny stories, exciting "wins" or depressing "losses." My skills had increased with experience, but William Betz could have been my first client or he could have been my last.

Chapter 8

THE NEXT DAY I pulled into the courthouse-jailhouse complex and parked my BMW at the western end of the lot beside the jail. A light drizzle fell slowly from dark clouds, making lower Manhattan seem grimmer than usual. The small, asphalt playground down the hill on the edge of Chinatown was deserted.

I walked toward the area between the courthouse and the jail, two equally tall brick buildings facing each other, twenty yards apart, separated by a marble terrace. Carrying my worn, leather briefcase, I climbed the steps to the terrace.

Usually when a case was over I stopped thinking about it, but that wasn't happening with the Betz trial, and it certainly wasn't happening in connection with my cross-examination of Lisa Altman. I couldn't seem to get out of my mind the image of that beautiful woman sitting vulnerably, helplessly in the witness chair.

I had other cases to distract me. My law practice was filled with clients who needed my attention. I knew I would have to move on.

"Lawyah Roehmah! Lawyah Roehmah!" a voice from inside the jail called out.

I looked up the face of the twelve-story jail. The building had the same narrow openings for windows as the courthouse, but instead of windows the openings of the jail were dark, wire-mesh screens. It was impossible to make out the black faces of inmates behind them.

"Lawyah Roehmer! I'm a trapestry of justice!" another voice from inside the jail called.

"Yo. Lawyah Roehmer! Hey Jewboy, ged me outta heah," still another voice yelled.

I made my way to the entrance of the jail. "Ah, prick me, do I not bleed?" I muttered under my breath.

I pulled hard on the heavy, blue-tinted, bulletproof glass door. Bright fluorescent lights lit up every corner of the lobby. I had been to dozens of prisons. Even the modern ones stored the inmates like animals in a kennel, a kennel where the inmates were regularly serviced with all their basic needs except heterosex. I hated prisons.

I stepped up to the next set of glass doors. I opened them, walked in, and exchanged nods with a guard I knew seated behind a desk in the lobby.

"How's it going, Tim?" I asked.

"It's a jungle out there, Mike. At least we're safe here."

We both smiled, and I walked over to the large control booth. Inside three guards were engaged in an animated conversation that I couldn't hear because of the thick glass that were the enclosure's walls. I took a three-by-five card from the pile on the metal shelf extending out from the booth. I wrote the name of the inmate on the card, dropped it in a metal drawer, and pushed the drawer until it extended inside.

A guard retrieved the card. He flipped through a black spiral book and walked over to an intricate intercom. Although I couldn't hear him, I knew he was calling to have my client brought down. He dropped the card back in the metal drawer and pushed it toward me. The guard cupped his ear with his hand and pointed to the six-inch, perforated silver disk implanted in the glass separating me from him.

I leaned toward the silver disk.

"You're lucky. The inmates just finished feeding," the guard said. "So it should only take a couple of minutes."

I nodded and picked up the card. After walking several feet to my left to a solid metal door, I waited for the guard to turn the switch. Finally he did. Small red bulbs flashed on the panel. A lock clanked loudly, and the metal door in front of me began to slide open, rasping loudly. I slipped sideways past the door as soon as the space was large enough, then marched forward fifteen feet to face a barred door. When the metal door behind me clanked shut, the barred door opened wide enough for me to slip through.

I walked another ten feet to confront a guard standing behind another barred door, and passed the three-by-five card through the bars to him. Without reading the card, he took a large heavy key and opened the door. I placed my briefcase on the floor next to a small table and signed my name into a guest book on the table. The guard used another large key to open a solid door. I entered the lawyers' conference room. The guard closed the door behind me.

In the beginning of my career, when I had first started going to prisons, I used to feel an excitement hearing the doors lock behind me as I entered the holding areas to interview clients. I had known, of course, that being locked up as an inmate was completely different from the temporary sense of constraint experienced by a lawyer making a brief visit. I had enjoyed meeting my clients, learning about the awful things they had done. In the beginning I had even been thrilled by the ugly prisons themselves.

My excitement about being in them, however, had quickly faded. Prison life was not something I had learned about in law school. But what I soon learned from spending so much time in prisons was terribly depressing. That's what was so upsetting about sentencings . . . like the sentencing the day before when Judge Fazio had sent my client, Sherry Parruco, away for years.

The airless, windowless conference room was about half the size of an average courtroom, made bright by the harsh fluorescent bulbs beaming down. Five-foot-high dividers formed a series of small cubicles on each side of the room. A narrow corridor separated the two rows of cubicles. Each cubicle contained a couple of unmatched chairs and an old desk.

I walked down the corridor. The first three cubicles were empty. In the fourth, a large black man with three tattooed teardrops running down the corner of one eye was looking earnestly at a young man sitting across from him, diligently writing on a yellow legal pad. The prisoner noticed me immediately. Prisoners get good at noticing even the flick of a finger from across a room. The young lawyer kept on writing as I passed.

I entered the last cubicle. I took off my jacket and placed it over a chair behind the desk and sat down. The desk was scratched and gouged.

"I swear it on my baby's eyes," I could hear the prisoner say.

"It had better be true. I'm going all out for you," the young lawyer said.

"I can't thank you enough," the prisoner said.

"Okay. We'll go to trial. I'll let the prosecutor know. Let's get out of here."

The young man and his client made their way to the door. I could hear a knock, and a moment later the guard opened the door to let them out. He relocked the door. I sat in my chair waiting for Jack Larsen and began to ruminate.

At the start of my practice, I used to speak to my clients just the way the young lawyer was speaking. I couldn't remember when it had begun to feel foolish to ask a client if he was innocent. I learned pretty quickly in my career that nearly every client lied to me. Most of the time it didn't matter what the client told me. If that guy in the cubicle was guilty—and most people in jail were—he probably was right to be lying. Young lawyers often worked harder for their clients if they thought they were preventing a miscarriage of justice.

William Betz had probably lied to me. Why would

he have been any different from most of my other clients? He might not have lied completely, but it was very likely that at least *some* of his testimony had been false. Did he rape Lisa? Who knew? I certainly didn't. I had never asked him if he had done it—I only asked him what he had told the police he had done.

A criminal lawyer was surrounded by a swamp of lies. Clients, witnesses, cops, prosecutors, even judges—everybody lied or could be lying. I tried to be an exception. I assuaged my conscience by "merely" shaving the truth, slanting the truth, avoiding the truth, which for a long time was enough of a nuance of a difference to convince myself that while I might be living in that swamp of lies, I still had my integrity, and had only used other people's lies to do my job.

For many years I simply ignored the fact that defendants lied, or, if I could not ignore it, I somehow forgave them for it. In a perverse way, I didn't feel their lying was as outrageous as other people in the criminal justice system doing it. Defendants, after all, were desperately trying to stay out of prison, and after having spent so much time as a visitor in prisons myself, I could sympathize with that desire.

If only Lisa weren't so attractive, I thought. "Those long, lovely legs should have carried her out of harm's way. And why am I starting to talk to myself in this godforsaken place?"

I had always seen the *defendants* as victims; that was my problem. For psychological reasons I didn't understand, I didn't hold my clients accountable for their behavior in the same way I would others. Their helplessness and dependence on me generated protective feelings, regardless of the crimes they might have committed. I needed to shield them from anyone who wanted to harm them—from the prosecutor, for example, and his array of cops and detectives and experts. And if a client was hostile toward me, my first reaction, on some level, had been to suspect he might be right to see me as part of an oppressive society, and I would even feel a vague guilt.

Now, as I waited in my cubicle for my client, I felt only impatience.

I wondered what the Altman woman—what Lisa— wanted from me. How long would she continue to follow me? I didn't feel threatened, at least not physically, but I knew I was going to call the police if I saw her around my house again. She had better stay the hell away from Molly, I said to myself. And what the hell was she doing in court?

But, although I had to admit it had been unnerving to see her when I'd looked over my shoulder, I'd somehow known I'd see her again.

I had always hoped that victims, or witnesses, or judges to whom I had done terrible things would understand that there was nothing personal in my behavior. I was just doing my job. I also knew that that was a bit too much to ask of most people. I was sure that Lisa didn't have the kind of detachment to appreciate that our system of jurisprudence required vigorous advocates.

I looked at my watch. How long, I wondered, would I have to wait for my criminal? I stood and walked up and down the narrow corridor.

A few minutes later I was waiting by the desk when the metal door clanked, then yawned open. I heard a shuffle of footsteps. A few moments later Jack Larsen, a handsome, muscular black man in his midthirties, arrived at the entrance of my cubicle. He was wearing bedroom slippers, dungarees, and an orange shirt.

I nodded at my client.

"Hi, Mr. Roehmer."

"Have a seat," I said.

My man sat down.

"Can you get my bail reduced, Mr. Roehmer? I want to get out of here. That's what I want."

"Jack, your bail is a hundred grand."

"But that's crazy. Can't you get it reduced?"

"How much can you afford?"

"Nothing. I gave you all the money I could get my hands on."

"There's no way you can get released without bail."

"This is my first charge."

"And it's for attempted murder."

"Without Perry," Larsen said, "all they got is Bruce's word against mine."

"That and a twelve-inch bread knife and eighty sutures in Bruce's stomach," I responded.

"But they ain't gonna find Perry."

"Careful, I don't trust these rooms."

"And you're gonna destroy that faggot, Bruce, right?" Larsen asked.

"I'll go as far as the judge lets me."

"But you're gonna destroy that faggot, right?"

"I'm going to try, but there's no guarantee I'll succeed."

"This place is going to make me crazy."

"I'm sorry, Jack. Your case should be coming up for trial in another month or two."

My client nodded.

"Anyway, I wanted to remind you not to talk to anybody about the case. And that goes for other inmates, guards, anybody. You haven't done that, have you?"

"No, sir. That's what you told me last time you saw me."

"Well, the main reason I wanted to see you today was to talk to you about a plea. Are you willing to consider it?"

"No. It's out of the question. That faggot had it coming."

"Do you understand that I might be able to get you a deal where you serve a year or two?"

"No deals. Bruce has friends down there. They'll kill me down there. No deals. You got to get me off."

"Okay. It's your decision. I'm required to ask you. I'll see you before we go to trial," I said.

"Thank you, Mr. Roehmer."

"If you change your mind about a plea, get in touch with me."

"I understand."

I stood, and Larsen stood up after me. We walked to the metal door. I tapped on it with a coin and waited. It seemed to take forever for the guard to come. My client was standing next to me, waiting for the same door to be unlocked, so that he could go back to his cell. I didn't look at him. In the past I had worked harder to do well for a client like Larsen than

I had for other, less violent clients. It was another way of demonstrating my distance from the horror of the crime and the criminal. Now I just wanted to get out of there.

Finally, the guard opened the door.

Chapter 9

THE FOLLOWING DAY I was in my office trying to move some paper off my desk when the intercom buzzed.

"Yes, Sylvia?" I asked.

"There's a Mr. Lanza on the phone. He says he's a client of yours."

"He's telling the truth. Armed robbery," I said.

"How come I don't know he's your client?"

"How come you're not Della Street?" I asked. "Could you please tell him I'll call him back, and I'd like not to take any calls right now. I got weeks of paperwork to catch up on. Thank you."

A moment later the intercom buzzed again.

"Yes, Sylvia?" I said with a sigh.

"There's a woman here who says she wants you to represent her."

I looked at my watch, looked at the mound of papers on my desk, and shook my head. "Please show her in."

A moment later the door opened and Lisa Altman entered.

I tried not to show any surprise.

"I was hoping I could speak to you," Lisa said.

I hesitated for a moment. Lisa Altman was about the last person I'd have expected as a visitor in my office—apparently wanting me to represent her. I gestured with my hand for her to sit down in the chair across from me.

"This is just the way I thought your office would look. Is that your daughter?" she asked, pointing to a photograph on top of a bookcase near my desk, taken two years ago, of Molly in a bathing suit, standing on a beach, and holding a bucket.

"What can I do for you, Ms. Altman?"

"Don't you think after all we've been through you could call me Lisa?"

I nodded and waited.

"I want you to represent me," she said.

I smiled. "Oh, really? What's the charge?"

"I assume they will accuse me of murder."

I became serious. "Why would you want me to represent you?"

"I know what you're capable of."

"Why do you think you'll be charged with murder?"

"I love the fact that you don't ask me if I committed the murder. That's very courtly of you."

"Thanks."

"Because I shot someone last night," she said matter-of-factly.

"Who?"

"An ex-client of yours."

"Yes?"

"William Betz."

I studied Lisa for a moment. "Have you told the police?" I asked.

"You're the only one I've told."

"Where did this shooting take place?"

"At his apartment. I imagine the body is still there."

"Why did you go to his apartment?"

"He forced me to go there. He told me he'd rape me again if I didn't go to his apartment."

"I have no intention of getting involved." I didn't even want to hear the details.

"You *are* involved."

"What do you mean?"

"If it hadn't been for you, I wouldn't have killed him."

"How's that?"

"If you hadn't gotten him off . . ." She paused for a moment. "He told me I didn't have a prayer that anyone would believe me a second time. He said you would destroy me again in court."

"Then what happened?"

"I shot him. Michael, he was right: you *would* have destroyed me again."

"You flatter me. You should see another lawyer."

"I want you."

"Sorry."

"After what you did to me in that courtroom, you owe it to me."

"I don't owe you anything. I won't take your case."

We stared at each other.

"Where did you get the gun?" I finally asked.

"I've been carrying it since the end of the trial. I knew he was going to come after me again."

"How did you know that?"

"The same way I knew he was following me the first time, before I even saw him."

I hesitated a moment. "I'll arrange to take you in. I'll try to get you a low bail. But that's it. Do you understand?"

"Yes."

"Then you'll have to get another lawyer. Okay?"

"Yes."

"Where can I reach you later in the day?"

"I have a rehearsal." She stood. "I think you know where it is."

I nodded. "Why were you outside my house the other night?" I asked.

"I was curious."

"I don't want you near my house again, understand?"

She nodded.

"And yesterday in court? What were you doing there?"

"I was watching you."

"How the hell did you know I would be there?"

"I called your office, and your secretary told me. When will I see you again?"

"This afternoon," I said.

Lisa rose and, without saying anything more, walked out of my office.

Chapter 10

I WAS SEATED in a row of orange, clamlike chairs. Two fat old black women were seated at the end of the row. I watched the receptionist, who was sitting behind a gray metal desk.

"I'm sorry for the delay," the receptionist said. "Mr. Phalen said he'd be out in a minute. I don't know what's taking him so long."

"Most of practicing law is waiting," I said. "I've gotten good at it. I'm sure he'll be out as soon as he can."

I looked over at the two women, who were also waiting. They sat silently, glaring at the receptionist. They could have been suspects, witnesses, or victims. There was nothing in their appearance that gave me a clue. They looked poor and angry, but that described most of the people who came in contact with the prosecutor's office.

I liked John. He was a good prosecutor, and he was

a gentleman. I had dealt with a number of honest and decent prosecutors over the years, but there were others I wouldn't have trusted under any circumstances.

I'd seen prosecutors violate legal ethics by telling me certain reports or witnesses didn't exist when they clearly knew otherwise. Other times, in an effort to pressure a plea, they'd told me they had more evidence or witnesses than they actually had. Some prosecutors encouraged cops to lie and told them what to say; some, more subtly, told the eager-to-be-helpful cop what would be the most effective testimony and only then asked him what had actually happened.

I hadn't felt that I had violated legal ethics or any personal moral code by anything that I had done during the Betz trial. Legal ethics allowed me as a defense lawyer to destroy a witness like Lisa Altman. The system allowed me to feel moral outrage at a prosecutor who knowingly misled me, but that didn't imply any ethical restraint on my humiliating in front of a jury a pathetic victim of a terrible crime! Something was wrong here.

I actually believed that there had been nothing personal in what I had done to Lisa, but if a prosecutor lied to me, I took it very personally—and I would wait for as long as it took to get even.

John Phalen finally entered the room. "Sorry, Michael," he said.

"No problem. We've got a lot to talk about," I said.

I followed John down a long corridor toward his office. We passed a line of cubicles, one of which I had occupied a number of years before. I looked inside, but no one was there. In the next one down I saw Cheryl seated at her desk. She had a long accordion file in front of her and a fat, middle-aged man seated across from her—Rocky Nisivoccia, or Fat Rocky, as some of his colleagues called him. Rocky had an overgrown crew cut that looked in need of a lawn mower.

I had known Rocky for years. In fact, he'd been assigned to me when I was a prosecutor. He had once told me a story about his daughter, Angela, that I'd never forgotten. When she was four, according to Rocky, she had had some kind of ear problem, and needed an operation. Rocky found the best ear specialist in the state. He took Angela to the hospital and waited outside the operating room. When the doctor came by on his way into the operating room, Rocky grabbed him by the shirt and pushed him up against the wall. According to Rocky, he said to the doctor, "Doc, I have five kids, all boys except my Angela. She's the youngest. She's my favorite. Understand? No mistakes." And the doctor said, "Yes, sir, Mr. Nisivoccia. No mistakes."

I loved Rocky's stories. They certainly hadn't taught those kinds of lessons about social engineering in law school.

"Hey, there's my main man," Rocky said, looking up at me as I paused at the doorway. Rocky always seemed pleased to see me.

I said hello to Cheryl and Rocky. "How're we doing on the Larsen case?" I asked.

"No problem," Rocky said, folding his short, fat fingers on the desk. "We're going to rid this city of miscreants one by one. How do you like that word, Mikey? *Miscreants*. Not bad, huh?"

"Great, Rocky," Cheryl said.

"I thought you were in homicide," I said.

"Yeah, I'm helping Angelo out. He's home nursing a bleeding ulcer. So not only is this not my case, the victim's alive, gay, and probably had it coming.

"That's what I love about you, Rocky," Cheryl said. "You have such a practical approach to the law."

"Are we going to start the Larsen case soon?" I asked. "My guy's still in jail."

"Sure. Sure. No problem," Rocky said.

Cheryl shrugged.

I said good-bye and moved on. I finally reached John's office. He was already seated behind his desk and I sat down across from him.

"Permit me to congratulate you again on the Betz rape," John said. "You did a good job, Michael."

"That's very gracious of you. I came off better than my client," I said.

"Only because you were lucky."

"Oh, really?"

"You had timing on your side," John said.

"Timing?"

"I got a call from a woman a couple of days after the verdict," John said. "Obviously it was too late for me to use it, but the woman told me that she'd also been raped by Betz."

"You couldn't have used it even if she had called before the verdict," I said.

"I might have been allowed. She said she was

followed and he pushed his way into her apartment, the same way he did with the Altman woman."

John was right: with those facts it was possible the judge would have regarded Betz's behavior as a pattern. "Well, why the hell did she wait until the trial was over? If she'd come forward earlier, maybe she could have nailed the fucker."

"She said she was frightened. And she thought he was going to be convicted without her. I can understand that."

"When did Betz rape that one?"

"She said it was about a year ago. She didn't want to give me any more details."

"Did she give you her name?" I asked, reflexively. She might be a helpful witness to Lisa in her murder trial. Then I remembered that I wasn't going to represent her. But I could pass the information on to her lawyer.

"No. She wouldn't give me her name. I pushed her for it, but she asked me if she came forward now would it make any difference, and I had to tell her that I didn't think so. What the hell was I supposed to do, lie to her?"

"No. You're right. By the time you were talking to her, it wouldn't have made any difference." John didn't realize the extent of the damage caused by this woman's not having come forward earlier.

"You got one lucky client," John said.

"He would have been luckier if he'd been convicted. I'll get to that. The public defender called me just before I started the Betz trial and asked me to take on the Williams murder. I haven't gone to prison yet to meet the guy, but I gather this is another case of yours."

John reached into his desk. He took out a large manila envelope and threw it at me. "I thought I'd seen the worst. Take a look at these cheesecakes," John said.

I opened the envelope and removed a dozen eight-by-ten glossy photographs. They were morgue shots of a little girl of about two years of age lying naked on a narrow, stainless-steel slab. Each picture had been taken from a different angle, some close-up, of the scars, the whip marks, the torn flesh.

When Carmen, the woman from the public defender's office who assigned the cases, had told me over the phone that my new client was charged with murdering his daughter, I had shrugged off my initial disgust at the thought of the horror of such a crime. I hadn't accepted the case yet, but I had felt curious, drawn to find out what normal restraints of decency were missing in this man.

"I . . . ," I started to respond, but I had nothing to say. "I . . . Goddamn. How can people do such things? Have they no souls?" I shook my head and shoved the pictures back into the envelope, which I threw at John.

In the past I would have had an intellectual curiosity about a client like Williams. Maybe it would have been a way of keeping some emotional distance from him. *Infanticide*. The very word sounded clinical—unconnected to the reality of a man battering his daughter to death.

"If you look closely, you can see the cigarette burns on her forehead," John said.

"Thanks anyway. I don't know if I can deal with this guy." In all the years I'd been practicing criminal law, I had never turned down a case. And Christ, for all that time I hadn't thought twice about taking on a client like Williams. But now . . . "To break my ass for a creep like that—I just don't know," I said. "I've saved enough guilty animals."

"Well, there's no law that says you have to. Just let me know."

"Give me a couple of days."

"There's something else?" John asked.

"Yeah. Some unfinished business from the Betz case."

"Oh?"

"I'm told his dead body might be rotting in his apartment," I said casually.

John paused for a moment. "I wouldn't sit shivah, as you folks say. Do we have a perpetrator?"

"I'd rather call her a suspect. I actually think this one's innocent, but I'm not sure I'm going to represent her, either.

"What? An innocent client and you don't want to take it? You were just complaining about breaking your ass for guilty animals."

"It's too complicated, John."

"Too much pressure to win if they're innocent?"

"There's some truth in that. But no, I'm thinking of getting out of the crime business altogether."

"The slime business. But what the hell would you do?"

"Maybe there's another area of the law," I said, sounding wistful.

"It'll bore you to death," he said.

"Maybe," I said.

"You know what Norman Dogbein once told me?" John asked.

"I'm sure I've heard it."

"He said, 'John, kid, when I'm trying a case, standing there in front of a jury, it's the only time I feel totally alive.' "

"I'm sure that's true for Norman," I said.

"Sure, but not for you?"

"Maybe."

"Maybe leaving the crime business after winning for an innocent client would be a good way to go out. Kind of like a redemption," John said.

"Sure."

"One kicker, of course: you're sure the innocent client's innocent?"

"Maybe," I said.

Chapter 11

I WALKED ACROSS the street to the theater. The lobby was empty of people. I pulled one door. It was locked. I tried another and entered.

I walked through the lobby into the theater and stood behind the barrier between the last row of seats and the open area at the back.

The curtains were drawn back. The houselights were dim, but the overhead stage lights were on. Some sets and props were leaning against the back wall of the empty stage. Someone I couldn't see was playing the piano in the orchestra pit.

I recognized Gene Carter. He was famous, a ferocious choreographer who was frequently mentioned in the reviews of Lisa's performances that I had just been rereading. He was sitting in the first row of the audience seats, loudly tapping a cane to the beat of the music.

After four taps of the cane, Gene said, "Okay. Now . . ."

Lisa entered from stage right with a series of ballet turns. She was dressed in a leotard and ballet shoes. With her hair pinned back severely, and wearing no makeup, she looked as if she had been rehearsing for a long time.

"Yes. Better. Better," Gene said.

Lisa did several turns.

"Stop," Gene said.

The piano music and Lisa stopped. Gene shook his head. He stood and walked with a limp to the stage.

"The turn. Repetition. Variation," Gene said, hitting his cane.

"I did that," Lisa said.

"No. The variation should be a break in tempo," Gene said, gesturing extravagantly with his hands.

"Right," Lisa said.

"Give me what *I* want. Understand?" Gene said.

Lisa nodded impatiently.

"Okay. Start from the jeté," Gene said.

Lisa took her position, and Gene remained at the edge of the stage. He beat his cane and the piano started up. Lisa began with a light jump, transferring her weight from one foot to the other.

"Softly. Softly," Gene instructed.

Lisa moved gracefully across the stage.

"Flowing. Easy," Gene said.

Lisa stopped after a few steps, then walked back to the spot where she had begun the last move.

"I'll begin again from here," Lisa said.

"Okay. It's beginning to look better," Gene said.

Gene beat the cane and the piano began again. Lisa

started the jump. This time she seemed to have more concentration.

"Yes. Yes," Gene said.

Lisa glided across the stage.

"Yes. Flowing. Ah. *Hit!*" Gene said, banging his cane hard against a seat. Lisa came to a dramatic halt. The tempo of the music increased and Lisa took off again with increased passion.

"Don't rush it," Gene said.

Lisa appeared more vulnerable.

"Yes. Open. Open," Gene said.

Gene seemed aroused and excited. He banged the cane with increasing ferocity. "Yes. Lovely," he said.

On one of the turns, Lisa's long hair came undone and flowed out behind her. She looked like a little girl.

"Now building. Ready for the entrechat . . . sharply. From the glissade," Gene said.

Lisa went into a new jump, crossing her feet rapidly at the highest point. There was a growing warmth in her performance.

"Again. Again," Gene said.

She repeated the jump.

"Again. Again. Sharper," Gene said.

Lisa jumped again, almost frantically.

"Moving. Yes," Gene said.

Lisa appeared almost in pain.

"Yes. Yes," Lisa whispered.

"Break. Now the battement! The battement!" Gene screamed, pounding his cane.

Lisa extended one foot from a fixed position against the lower calf of the supporting leg, then brought the foot back hard, almost hitting it. She repeated the move over and over, furiously, each time lifting herself up on the toe of the supporting foot.

"Harder! Again! Harder!" Gene screamed.

Lisa threw her arms outward each time she lifted herself up on her toe. She seemed possessed, transported.

"That's it," Gene said coldly.

Gene put down the cane and clapped his hands.

The man playing the piano stood up and walked out of the room. Gene put his papers together on a nearby table. Lisa tried to pull herself together. She was breathing hard.

"That's probably as good as you can do it," Gene said.

"Thanks," Lisa said, sarcastically.

"You're getting harder to crank up," Gene said.

"You're getting harder to bear," Lisa said.

"A couple of more lines around the eyes, my dear, and you'll be on your knees for me," Gene said.

"I'd kill myself first," Lisa said, and picked up a sweater thrown over a chair. She wrapped herself in it and walked off the stage.

I stepped out of the darkness at the back of the theater and hurried down the aisle, then opened the door and climbed the steps to the back of the stage.

I saw Lisa walking slowly down the corridor. From her gait, she seemed exhausted, dejected, and very much alone. She was wiping her face and neck with a towel.

I walked down the corridor after her. There were dressing rooms on both sides. She reached her room and entered. I walked to that door. I opened it and entered.

The room was spare and typical. No windows. The dressing table was strewn with small objects. A large, stuffed overnight bag was on the floor beside the dressing table. Lisa was seated at the table, taking off her ballet shoes. Still sweating, she had the towel around her neck.

"After all the descriptions of this place at the trial, I feel I've been here before," I said.

"This room wasn't described at the trial," Lisa said, without turning.

"You're right. It was my investigator's report."

"So where do we stand?" Lisa asked. She wiped her face and neck with the towel and threw it on the dressing table.

"I talked to the prosecutor."

"And?"

"He's probably at Betz's apartment now."

"What happens next?" Lisa watched me from the mirror in front of her.

"You go in for bail," I said.

"I can't put up much money."

"What do you mean?"

"I don't have it," she said, still looking at my reflection in the mirror.

"What do you mean you don't have it? You're one of the most successful dancers in the country. What do you do with your money?"

"I had someone manage my money, and he managed to lose it all and not pay my taxes. Everything I earned in the last two years has been taken by the government."

"I might be able to get you out without bail."

"How can you arrange that?"

"The prosecutor told me that the day after Betz was acquitted a woman contacted him. She told him that Betz had also raped her."

"Did he believe her?" Lisa asked, finally turning around to look at me directly.

"Yes."

"Why?"

"I suppose it was because she has no reason to lie."

"Do you believe her?"

"Yes."

"Why her and not me?"

"I never said I didn't believe you."

"You tried to make a liar out of me in front of the jury."

"Testing your credibility, it's called."

"Why didn't she come forward before?"

"She was frightened. She probably thought he'd be convicted without her having to go through the ordeal of a trial."

"I can sympathize with that."

"The prosecutor told me he wouldn't fight a relatively low bail," I said.

"Why not?"

"He probably feels guilty he wasn't able to convict Betz."

Lisa stood and walked toward me. She came face-to-face with me, inches away. Her face was still wet with the sweat from her rehearsal. Her hair was disheveled.

"And you? How do you feel?" Lisa asked.

"I feel no guilt."

"Why not?"

"I was just doing my job," I said.

"What about now? Will you do your job for me?"

I stared at her.

"Let me show you something that might convince you," she said.

I stood amazed as Lisa pulled off her leotard from one shoulder, and then the other. She pulled it down to her waist, uncovering smooth, beautiful breasts. She continued pulling the leotard down to her hips. I saw that she had terrible scratches running down her stomach.

"Where did you get those scars?" I asked.

"That's where your client scratched me when he ripped off my blouse."

"Why didn't you tell me about that before?"

"I was going to tell you."

"We'll have to get photographs. This will be crucial at the trial."

"Then you'll represent me?"

I hesitated for a moment.

"Counselor, I've put a question to you," she said.

"I know."

"I direct you to answer the question."

"Let me think about it," I said.

She was beautiful. She reached over and flipped off the switch to the lights. A light from the bathroom threw enough illumination for me to see her silhouette. She stepped closer to me, and reached out gracefully and began stroking the side of my face.

I finally responded by kissing her, at first gently, then more aggressively. She pulled back from me playfully, then came closer to me, teasing me, and then pulled back again. I stepped toward her. She backed up. I advanced. It was almost like a dance, in which she was leading me over to the couch, where we finally embraced. We kissed passionately, deeply, intensely. I eased her down onto the couch. And there we made love.

Chapter 12

WHEN I LEFT Lisa in her dressing room, I got my car out of the garage near the theater and went for a ride. I didn't have any destination, I just wanted to calm down for a while. I headed downtown, and without really planning any route found myself in the Holland Tunnel, and then I was on the Pulaski Skyway, heading toward Newark.

Lisa was the first client I'd ever had sex with. I knew it wasn't such an unusual event for a lawyer; Norman had boasted of his many conquests. It was unethical, but that wasn't the reason I'd not done it before. I simply hadn't cheated on Jenny through all the years we had been together. And I would have resisted Lisa today if Jenny hadn't walked out on me. There—now I felt I had yet another grievance against Jenny. "It was her fault I made love to Lisa," I said out loud in the car, knowing full well that my accusation was preposterous.

Lisa was some beautiful piece of work. I knew deep in my bones that getting involved with her was a mistake. I felt I was losing control, and that scared me a lot. It also thrilled me. I was sure that at some point down the road, I was going to regret taking her case on . . . and taking *her* on.

I stopped my car in front of a three-story brick apartment house. I hadn't been there in almost thirty years. Across the street was a solid brick wall that was the back of a movie theater. I noticed the faint brown outline of a rectangle—the two-by-three-foot strike zone we'd created for our stickball games when I was a kid. My mother used to watch me from the second-floor kitchen window.

I looked at the window, but it was dark inside. From the time I was about eight years old until I was about fourteen, I would periodically give my mother a home permanent in that kitchen—a "Toni," it was called. She would sit at the kitchen table and I would roll her hair up in curlers. I would wrap a small, very thin piece of paper around each curler, then slip a bobby pin into it. Then I would dab a vile-smelling liquid on the curled-up hair. I had never smelled the odor of that liquid before those permanents and never have since. My mother was always very appreciative of my helping her. "Such a good boy," she would always say. I now missed the smell of the Toni.

Later that evening, sometime after nine, I arrived at my house. When I wasn't on trial, I usually got home before Molly went to sleep at about seven, but I hadn't been paying attention to the time.

As I entered the hall, I noticed a light on in the

living room. Jenny was seated on the sofa, reading. Almost every day of the week, Jenny spent time with Molly when she came home from school, but she usually left for her new apartment before I got home. I didn't expect her to be at the house now. She looked up from her book.

"Hi, Michael," Jenny said. "I let Judith go to a movie and put Molly to bed myself."

I took off my jacket and threw it over a chair.

"I didn't expect you back so late," she said. "We could have had dinner."

I walked toward her.

"Is there something wrong? I thought you'd be pleasantly surprised to see me."

I grabbed her hand, pulling her up onto her feet; her book fell to the floor.

"Well, hello," she said.

I held both her hands behind her back as I pressed my body up against her.

"What are you doing, Michael?" Jenny asked, trying to resist.

I tried to kiss her, but she squirmed away. I held her tight. She stopped squirming and stared at me. This time she let me kiss her, and I kissed her passionately.

"Michael, stop," Jenny said.

I led her over to the sofa. She became responsive. I unbuttoned her blouse, fumbling, almost ripping it off her shoulders. I unsnapped her bra.

"It's been so long," Jenny said.

I lifted up her skirt and pulled off her panties. I hurriedly undid my pants. And then I feverishly made love to her.

We remained on the sofa together after we had made love. I lay on my back, staring at the ceiling.

"I remember now how sometimes when we made love, I thought you were so angry," Jenny said.

I pulled up my pants and refastened my belt, then lay down on the sofa beside her again.

"We had so many wonderful times in bed, didn't we?" she asked, sitting up to fasten her bra and button her blouse.

"Yes," I said as I lit a cigarette and took a drag. "Wonderful times."

"Particularly after a trial," she said with a sly smile, lying back down beside me.

"Right. I was a regular hunter home from the hunt." I regretted immediately sounding sarcastic. "Jenny," I said.

"Yes?"

"I'm tired of feeling like such an outsider."

"Maybe you've been 'the killer in the courtroom' too long."

"I think so. Yes," I said.

"I . . . I've got to go," Jenny said. She stood up, tucked in her blouse, and straightened out her skirt.

I watched her putting on her panties.

"Will you walk me to the car?" she asked.

"Sure."

We headed toward the door.

"I feel a little shaky," she said. "This is the first time I've made love in a year. Not just with you— with anybody."

I nodded.

"Michael, this doesn't change anything, you know."

"I know." I paused a moment. "I tried to call you this afternoon," I said. "Bear died."

"I'm sorry, Michael."

As we reached her car, Jenny turned to me. "Is that why you made love to me, Michael? Because Bear died?"

"Of course not," I said.

After I watched Jenny drive away, I went upstairs. As I headed down the hallway toward my bedroom, I stopped at the door to Molly's bedroom.

I opened the door and entered quietly. I walked over to the bed and studied my daughter as she slept deeply and innocently. She was on her back, with her arms outstretched above her head. The bed looked way too big for her.

I bent down and placed my finger in her opened hand. She didn't awaken, but she grasped my finger and held it tight. I felt deep love for her. Molly was the only person in the world whom I loved without complication or reservation.

After a moment I pulled my finger out. I tucked the blanket in under the mattress, then leaned over and kissed her forehead. She opened her eyes.

"I'm sorry, Pumpkin. I didn't mean to wake you up," I said.

"That's all right," she said.

"You go back to sleep."

"Are you okay, Daddy?"

"I'm fine, sweetheart. I love you."

"Is that still all that matters?"

"You bet it is."

"Good." She rolled over and was asleep instantly.

I pushed back the fine hair beside her temples and kissed her forehead again. I watched her for another moment and then left.

Chapter 13

THE CONNECTICUT COUNTRYSIDE was lovely, gray and solemn. The only sounds were the wind and the creaking of the bare branches of bending trees. It was November, but as cold as winter, cold but with no snow. In the distance the rolling hills were in varying shades of dark brown and purple.

The grave site was on a knoll surrounded, as with a collar, by a low stone wall. The last rusty beams of sun bounced off a pond, small and frozen, about fifty yards away. The gray trees looked as if their color had been sucked from them by the cold earth. Their small branches, bare of leaves, were like spikes scratching the brutal wind as it passed.

The men wore dark suits and overcoats; the women were in fur coats and high heels. Jenny, Charles and Eleanor, Stan and Pebble, John Phalen, Cheryl Hazelton, and Judges Bennett, Taylor, and Fazio were part of the cluster of about twenty people gathered around the open grave.

The earth was hard, and the coldness seeped through my shoes and up through the bones of my body. I was standing at the edge of the grave, next to Bear's family: his wife, Margaret, who had always treated me like a son, and their two daughters, both of whom were older than I and whom I hardly knew.

The priest had already spoken for a few minutes, and the casket had been lowered. I looked down for a moment. We had been to the church first, and the service at the grave was supposed to be brief. I felt very self-conscious speaking at a Catholic service, but Margaret had asked me to say a few words, and I couldn't refuse her. I had always felt like an outsider, and it seemed particularly preposterous for me to be involved in this moment—preposterous on every level except for the fact that I had loved Bear as a father.

"Lloyd Singer, whom most of us knew as 'Bear,' hated sentimentality," I finally said as I began the eulogy. "He would have been pleased to use such an occasion to talk about what he cared about most: justice. Twenty-five years on the bench. He suffered so much at the end. That hardly seemed like justice."

I looked away. That wasn't at all the way I had wanted to begin.

Once, in my eagerness to understand how Bear's religious beliefs supported his commitment to what he did on the bench, I had gladly accepted his invitation to attend a Jesuit retreat. During the prayer services I had watched him speak to his God with deep devotion, and I learned that he attended church every morning. Up to that point, which was near the end of my year of clerking, I'd had no idea that he was so religious. When I had asked him if he felt his commitment to love and forgiveness created any personal conflict with his work as a judge, he said he had no difficulty reconciling his religious and professional lives. He believed he was doing important work in trying to balance society's interest in deterring criminal behavior with its commitment to protect the rights of those accused of a crime. I had always felt it was a pity I didn't have his religious convictions.

"Many of us in the course of a day make decisions of consequence," I started again, "but society has given to a few the right to decide matters affecting the lives and sometimes even the deaths of strangers. People very much like the rest of us exercise this astonishing and terrible power when they serve as judges. By agonizing over their decisions—or by avoiding or repressing such agony—judges develop a special way of looking at the world, at the value of life, and at the significance of death.

"Judges are, of course, engaged in issues of justice and process, but I'm talking here about human beings who are making awful, fateful decisions about other human beings, and the effect such responsibility has on the people who exercise it—an effect that is sometimes corrosive, sometimes humbling, and sometimes ennobling.

"Bear lived his life with integrity, not only by scrupulously following legal ethics, but also by his own moral compass—somehow finding a way to reconcile the two. That's not always easy. To act honorably, with self-respect. That was the way he managed to live his life. He was honest with his family—his wife, to whom he was faithful for over thirty-five years, and his two children, whom he cherished. He knew that the sum worth of our lives was defined by the way we choose to spend our days, our moments . . . Integrity . . ."

I turned to Jenny, who was standing a few feet from me. "His work as a judge confronted him daily with the worst behavior of humanity. To remain committed to improving the human condition in the face of so much evidence of bestiality, without allowing that constant exposure to turn you into an embittered or unfeeling human being—the risk is not simply burnout," I said. I was looking at Jenny more than at any of the other people present, but I was speaking more to myself than to anyone else. "That would trivialize the real conflict. It's reconciling larger principles, like commitment to a justice system, with more personal moral convictions about the need to take responsibility for the consequences of one's own actions in a particular case."

I knew that most people around the grave of my friend wouldn't understand what I was talking about.

"Some criminal lawyers," I said, "like some of their clients, want to be above the law. They look for any slack in the legal rope attempting to bind their clients. To such lawyers, what counts is their performance, what they can get away with. At their core, these lawyers think the system is a fraud; they believe that their job is to deceive. Success for them is all sleight of hand. They interpret a jury's guilty verdict as evidence that they have been exposed as charlatans. When they lose, they see themselves as foolish dandies, inflated with self-importance and bravado, posturing with boutonnieres in their lapels and bright handkerchiefs in their breast pockets. Sometimes I have seen myself like this; Bear, never.

"Bear was my friend," I pushed on. "When he presided in a courtroom, he commanded respect and attention from everyone present. Sure he could be tough, but his control over a courtroom was the envy of every judge in the courthouse. A frown from him could bring a crowd to silence without his even uttering a word. If he ever had to raise his voice or bang his gavel, it was always clear to anyone who knew him that there was nothing personal in his behavior.

"Knowing that he was around, available for advice and reassurance, was a source of emotional support and strength. It's hard to imagine him not being there for me anymore. I loved him dearly. And I will miss him very much. . . . Many of us start out with lofty ideals, but somehow, along the way, the harshness of life and our chosen profession, the large and small cruelties, brutalize us. There is a nobility in holding on to ideals over a lifetime. . . . It's so hard . . ."

I again looked over at Jenny. My tears flowed not just from the loss of my mentor, but also from the realization that I had strayed so far from the ideals with which I had begun my career . . . and my marriage.

Jenny nodded toward me, almost imperceptibly, as if to say she understood.

After the service was over, I walked toward Jenny, but several people from the courthouse stopped me along the way. I shook hands with the judges. Judge Bennett reminded me that he and Bear had been roommates in law school, and that Bear had often spoken to him of me. Bennett told me that if I ever wanted to reminisce about Bear, we should get together. Cheryl Hazelton told me that she understood my loss, and hugged me briefly. I saw John Phalen and walked over to him.

"That was a fine eulogy, Michael," John said. "I know you'll miss the guy."

"Thank you." I signaled to Jenny that I would be with her in a moment.

On the way to the funeral, I had come to a decision about the case of the father accused of killing his two-year-old daughter. I assumed he was guilty. If I tried to help him, it would be out of habit or instinct, in the same way I might try to keep a vicious dog from being shot. But even if a vicious dog should not be shot, it should perhaps be restrained, I had decided. This potential new client had become a symbol to me of all the other clients I had represented over the years whom I'd hated without ever being able to admit it to myself.

For years, for all my career as a criminal lawyer, I would have represented him because it was my job as a lawyer to do so: "Someone has to represent him" . . . "Everyone is entitled to the best defense" . . . and the rest of the cant I had so often heard myself repeat.

When the public defender's office had called me about this case, I hadn't expected the assignment to trouble me. If I found a case or client so upsetting that my ability to function was impaired, I was permitted by legal ethics to withdraw—in fact, I was required to withdraw. But I knew that I *could* function as a good lawyer for Williams. I simply didn't *want* to represent him. But that hardly seemed a professional reason for quitting the case.

The question of emotional and moral responsibility for my actions was beginning to dominate my thoughts. I was concerned about the moral legitimacy of my own behavior in ways I had never even considered before. It was disturbing to think that the "rightness" of my actions depended somehow on the "rightness" or "wrongness" of my client's actions.

As I had imagined working on the case of the child-killer, I couldn't help hearing, once again, those accusing voices, like my next-door neighbor, Stan, or even Jenny, who so frequently asked: "Don't you take any responsibility for what you do? Don't you feel guilty if someone you get off goes out and commits another terrible crime?" I was no longer able to answer no and brush the thought aside. "I was only doing my job" was beginning to sound like a Nazi affirmation, but the comparison should have been ridiculous: I did what I did because I still believed our legal system was better than any other I knew of. Bear would have told me that now, as he had so often when he was alive.

But I couldn't stand the prospect of helping a father who had brutally murdered his own daughter. What if I somehow got him off, and he went out and killed someone else? I had to accept the moral responsibility for my actions, even if legal ethics gave me permission not to. As long as I had been able to think of myself as a mere technician performing a surgical procedure

("What the patient did after the operation was not my responsibility"), I was able to pass off the responsibility onto a parent, a social worker, or a clergyman, or even onto some vague notion of "society at large." I couldn't do that anymore.

"John, I've got to talk to you about that Williams case," I said.

"Yeah, isn't that something?" John said.

"It's too much. I just can't do it. The public defender's got to find someone else to represent him," I said.

"You didn't hear about it?" John asked.

"Hear what?"

"He was killed last night in the jail."

"What! No, I didn't hear about it. How did it happen?"

"They cut him. I don't know how they got to him. It's being investigated."

"The public defender said he was supposed to be in isolation."

"Ten stab wounds in the guy. I guess some defense lawyer is going to claim it was suicide."

"Pathetic."

"Not so pathetic. It's just one less scumbag," John said.

"Let me talk to you about it some other time," I said. It was clear that at this point neither John nor I gave a damn about the late child-killer.

"I'll see you tomorrow when you bring in the ballerina."

"Right."

I made my way to Jenny, and we slowly walked to our cars. She put her arm around me, comforting me.

"It took me years to get over the death of my parents," I said.

"Michael, I don't think you've *ever* gotten over that. You spent a good part of your life trying to protect them."

"I tried."

"And when they died, you somehow felt that you'd failed them," she said.

"I know. And I feel I failed Bear in the same way. I know it's crazy. God knows how long I'll mourn his leaving me."

"We all have to learn how little control we have over our lives," she said.

I stopped and hugged her. "You know, Jen, besides everything else, you're really a pal."

"You mean you don't want to kill me anymore for abandoning you?" Jenny asked.

"Maybe only a little," I said.

Chapter 14

THE DAY AFTER the funeral I was in my office. I told Sylvia to open a new client's file for Lisa Altman.

"I don't think you should be taking on that case," Sylvia said to me, the tone in her voice reminiscent of the way my mother would talk to me when I threatened to go outside in the rain without my galoshes.

"Well, I'm sorry, Sylvia. I seem to have already made the decision to take it on," I said defiantly. "Do you have a problem with that?"

"It doesn't look right. The man she murdered was your client."

"That she *killed*, there's no doubt. Whether she acted in self-defense will be up to the jury to decide."

"I still don't think it looks right. There's something wrong about it."

"Sylvia, you hate *most* of my clients," I said.

"Right. Most of them *are* bums."

"Well, I actually think Lisa is innocent. And regardless of whether she is or not, I've decided to represent her." Actually, I had come to my decision that morning as I was driving to my office. Up to that point I had only committed to take her in for booking and the setting of bail.

An hour later I picked up Lisa at her apartment. Parking downtown was always such a problem that I took a taxi. I had the car wait outside as I walked up the stoop of her building and pressed the bell to her apartment. A few minutes later Lisa came to the front door of the building. She was dressed in a brown silk suit and a navy blue blouse. She wore no jewelry and no makeup.

"How do you feel?" I asked as she stepped outside.

"This is not a role I ever wanted to play," she said. "I'm in your hands now . . . again."

We walked down the stoop. I held open the door to the taxi and got in after her. We didn't speak for the first few blocks as we headed downtown.

"There shouldn't be any surprises," I finally said. "I've set it all up with the prosecutor."

Lisa nodded. She was clearly nervous, but I admired how much in control she seemed. "I saw the article in the newspaper," she said.

The day before, the day of Bear's funeral, there had been newspaper reports of William Betz's death, and how his body had been found in his apartment. The articles quoted the head of homicide as saying that an arrest was imminent. Someone known to the decedent was about to be arrested and charged with murder. It hadn't said that Lisa was that "someone."

"It could have been a lot worse," I said.

"How?"

"It could have mentioned your name as the suspect, and it could have said you were coming in this morning. Then we would have had a mob of reporters and photographers."

"You always look at the bright side?"

"I try to. You'll be going in without handcuffs. And you'll sail through the whole process."

John had promised me he would meet us down at the courthouse and shepherd her through the fingerprinting and mug shots. John also promised me he would not oppose my application that she be released on her own recognizance, without having to put up any bail. I had explained all this to Lisa. She hadn't seemed particularly pleased by what I told her, or particularly grateful, but that was probably because she had no idea how degrading and terrifying the procedure could be to someone who wasn't a hardened criminal.

We were traveling after the morning rush hour, and there wasn't much traffic. We got down to the courthouse a few minutes before ten, the time I had arranged to meet John. Fortunately he was already in the homicide office and we didn't have to wait. I was able to stay with Lisa while she was fingerprinted. The police officer held her fingers one at a time, moving each quickly from the black ink pad to the white cardboard and rolling the blackened finger in the appropriate box. The man in charge of taking the prints was very experienced, and he was gentle with Lisa.

Lisa and I moved on to another cubicle for her mug shot to be taken. There a police officer arranged the letters of her name on a slate, then placed the beaded silver chain holding the board around her neck. He had her stand in front of a white screen. Out of reflex, I supposed, Lisa looked deeply into the camera and gave a slight smile as she was photographed.

"These aren't publicity stills," I joked as the police officer removed the board with her name.

"Well, you don't want a bad image floating around," she answered. She was quite cool about the process, but that was only possible because the cops were being unusually respectful.

About an hour later, Lisa and I entered a large courtroom, one that was older and seedier than the room where Lisa had testified in Betz's trial. Paint was peeling from the ceiling, and the walls were filthy. A number of people were sitting in the spectator seats. Six guards were standing in different parts of the room. The court clerk was seated at his desk in front of the empty judge's bench.

I told Lisa to take a seat near the front of the spectators' section of the courtroom, then walked over to the clerk. "How you doing, Sidney?" I said.

"Hi, Michael. We got a zoo here," the balding, middle-aged man in the gray suit responded.

"I'm sure you've got it under control," I said.

"I'm going nuts," Sidney said. "The cage in the back is bursting."

"What's the story?" I asked.

"There was a Puerto Rican riot. We got three cops in the hospital. One of them's serious."

I nodded. I walked to the right, opened the door leading to the holding pen, and entered.

A floor-to-ceiling wire-mesh screen divided the back half of the large room from the front half, where guards and lawyers were milling about. Behind the screen, eight men were sitting on a bench in various frozen positions, and several more were standing with their fingers clutching the wire mesh.

I walked up to the screen. Sidney was right—the cage was fuller than I'd ever seen it. A man was hunched over at the end of the bench; he turned to stare at me as I approached. He seemed terribly frightened. His badly bruised and swollen face looked like a bashed-in eggplant. One eye was hidden behind puffed-up flesh.

If Lisa had seen the grotesque scene just behind the courtroom, she would have fallen apart. I turned and walked out of the room.

I walked back to the clerk. "Sidney, can you do me a favor? Would you call me sooner rather than later? I've got to get back to my office." The truth was that I didn't want Lisa to have to witness the grinding, depressing parade of defendants who would be marched through the court that morning.

"Sure, Michael. What do you got going here?"

"A bail. There shouldn't be any problem."

"Oh, really?" Sidney sounded dubious, because he knew there was almost always *some* problem.

"The prosecutor's got no objection to a release on her own recognizance."

"Sounds good. Don't worry, Michael, I'll take care of you. Oh, and I wanted to thank you again for what you did for my daughter."

"Don't mention it. How's she making out?"

"She's working at the rehab center now. And she's been clean for over a year."

"That's great. By the way, who's on the bench?" I asked.

"Milt Rice."

"That's lucky," I said. Milt and I had worked together in the prosecutor's office over twenty years ago.

I walked back to where Lisa was seated.

The courtroom was more crowded than before. Lawyers and guards were standing around. Family and friends of the different defendants who'd be called were seated on the benches. A door on the opposite side of the judge's bench opened. Judge Rice entered the courtroom.

"All rise," Sidney said. "All those with business before this honorable court come forward, and you shall be heard. Judge Milton R. Rice presiding."

Judge Rice moved up the two steps and took his seat on the bench, then looked around the courtroom and noticed me. He nodded at me, and I nodded back. We had always gotten along well.

"Please call the first case, Sidney," Judge Rice said.

"State versus Lisa Altman," Sidney called out. He looked over at me and winked. I smiled my thanks back at Sidney.

I told Lisa to accompany me, and we walked over to the counsel table, where we stood side by side. John got up from his chair at counsel table, and we all faced the judge.

"How are you, Michael?" Judge Rice asked.

"Struggling with the elements, as always, Judge. It's good to see you."

"What brings you to our humble lower court?" Judge Rice asked with a smile.

I explained to the judge that although the charge was murder, the unusual circumstances of the case—the previous trial, Lisa's reputation in her field, the fact she had come forward voluntarily—meant that there was no likelihood of her fleeing the jurisdiction and not showing up for trial. John, as promised, told the judge that he had no objection to releasing her without bail, a fact that particularly persuaded the judge.

Lisa and I left the courthouse in less than an hour. It couldn't have been easier. Lisa had no idea how awful it all could have been for her.

Part II ⚖

Chapter 15

IT WAS THREE months later—three months during which I had seen Lisa several times a week; three months during which I had fallen in love with her. It had caught me totally by surprise. I was in love—passionately, childishly in love.

At first, it had troubled me a little that she was only twenty-nine, fifteen years younger than I. But she was certainly a grown-up. If anything, she was more world-worn and cynical than most women twice her age. The only thing that betrayed her youth was her tight, hard body . . . and that thrilled me and made me feel young again.

It was not entirely a comfort to learn from her that she had always gone out with older men.

Feeling out of control was frightening for me, probably more so than for most people. But the madness, the emotional chaos of it was also exhilarating. I was sure that this first, real experience of

143

wild, romantic love was also my last chance at it. It had occurred to me that my feelings might well have been heightened by the knowledge that what I was doing was wrong and dangerous. Wrong because the rules of legal ethics clearly stated that I should not be having an affair with a client. And dangerous because if anyone in the legal establishment found out about it, I could face disbarment. Bear would have been appalled. But for the time being, I felt I had no choice but to play it out.

And not surprisingly, I had finally stopped thinking about Jenny—I had stopped being obsessed with her absence when I woke up, and I had stopped longing for her in the evenings. I spoke much less frequently to Jenny by phone and rarely saw her now when she would visit with Molly at my house. She was taking Molly at all the agreed-upon times, but I hadn't been around for the pickups and deliveries, as I had in the past. Judith had been taking care of that.

Not seeing Molly during this period as often as I had before I'd fallen in love with Lisa was a real source of guilt. I was still taking Molly every other weekend and making those times special: museums, the zoo, puppet shows. But I was away much more than I'd ever been before. I had convinced myself that my absences were just for the period until the trial was over, that then I'd make some decision to tell Molly about Lisa—once I knew what to tell her. In the meantime, I never brought Lisa to the house, and never spoke to Molly about Lisa. Maybe there was some other reason why I was reluctant to have Molly meet Lisa, but I wasn't aware of it at the time. And

Lisa had the understanding and sensitivity never to ask to go to my house or to meet my daughter.

The three months had also been a time during which I became convinced that Lisa had killed Betz in self-defense. I was sure she was innocent of deliberately murdering Betz.

Lisa had no idea what prison was like or what it would do to her if she were convicted, and of course, there was no point in frightening her by telling her. I, on the other hand, couldn't get the nightmare of Lisa in prison out of my mind. I kept imagining her being terrorized there—being cursed at or beaten by the guards. I had a recurring memory of the Puerto Ricans in the cage behind the courtroom when I'd taken Lisa to court to set bail. I was glad she had never seen that.

There was another risk if Lisa went to prison. Not being street-toughened like my usual female clients, she wouldn't stand a chance of fighting off the inevitable sexual assaults by the other women inmates. If Lisa were convicted and sent to prison, she would immediately be thrown together with a terrifying mob of dangerous criminals—some of whom had been my clients. I desperately wanted to protect her, to save her from the ordeal of a trial, to avoid even the risk of a conviction.

During these three months, whenever we were together, we spoke only briefly about the case, and sometimes not at all. I had learned the basic facts of her background early on, in conversations that she later told me felt more like cross-examinations: she was twenty-nine years old; born in a small town in Iowa; had no brothers or sisters; had won a bout with polio by sheer grit and discipline. Her hardworking parents had somehow managed to pay for her early dance instruction, and scholarships and odd jobs had financed the rest of her training. She had never been married, never even lived with a man—and she had no interest in women.

Learning what Lisa was *really* like occurred more slowly. We were not unlike each other in our reluctance or inability to reveal ourselves to another person—and that was one reason we were drawn to each other. I didn't know when I had first admitted to myself that I loved her. It was probably pretty early on. She struggled with the fact that she needed me to defend her—it was about the only aspect of her life in which she wasn't totally in command. Only when we were making love did I see the same vulnerability in her. In every other respect she was totally self-reliant and independent. The discipline she brought to her dance, a kind of tunnel focus, carried over to almost every other part of her life. It pained her to admit that she needed me. And that excited *me* greatly.

I was in my office doing research on Lisa's case, studying recent court opinions from around the country in cases in which women had defended themselves against men who had abused them in the past. Papers and law books were piled on top of my desk, and I was determined to process a lot of this material, to get down to the wood of my desktop. That was my goal: to see wood. I had just settled in when the intercom buzzed.

"A young gentleman is here to see you," Sylvia's

voice said. "A Peter Brown. He's a couple of minutes early for his appointment, but he says it's important."

I had completely forgotten that Peter Brown had called the week before. He had told me he desperately needed to see me, but had refused to tell me what it was about. I had little interest in new cases, having become totally preoccupied with preparing for Lisa's trial. But practicing law was a business, among other things, and if I wanted to stay in business, I had to take on more clients. Lisa had said she had no money for bail, so I had assumed that she didn't have the money to pay me a fee, and I had never asked her for one. Maybe, if and when I won her case, I would give her a bill. In the meantime, I knew I had better speak to new clients.

"Okay. Okay. Ask him to come in," I said.

"It would be my pleasure," Sylvia's voice said.

"Sylvia, please see if you can locate Lisa Altman and get her on the phone. I've got to talk to her."

A moment later a man looking to be in his late thirties entered. He was wearing a navy blue suit that was a bit tight on him, black horn-rimmed glasses, and a crew cut that needed a trim. I shook hands with Peter Brown and gestured with my hand for him to have a seat.

The man sat down in the chair across from me.

"So?" I said, weary over the prospect of hearing about new problems. Everyone in the world had problems, and recently there'd been times when I felt that if I stayed any longer in this business I would hear all of them. But I didn't want to hear all of them.

"So?" the man answered.

"So what brings you here?" I picked up a pencil

and prepared to take notes. Already I didn't like the guy.

"You don't waste any time, do you?"

"I try not to," I said. The research to be done in Lisa's case was spread out on my desk, and I felt anxious to get back to it.

"I want you to know that I come from a family of great wealth."

"Good for you," I said, trying to sound earnest.

"And I'm prepared to pay you handsomely, up front, in cash."

"Good for me," I said.

"I read about you in the newspapers when you defended that man accused of raping that ballet star."

"That was months ago. What can I do for you?"

"I'm being harassed by the police. It's part of a terrible conspiracy. I want you to put an end to it."

"How do you know that it's part of a conspiracy?" I asked.

"I hear them talking to each other. I have like a transmitter in my mouth."

"In your mouth?"

"About two years ago I had some bridgework done. Ever since then I've been able to pick up messages," he said.

Without showing any reaction, I studied Peter Brown. "How old are you?" I asked.

"Forty-five."

"You look younger. So for the last couple of years you've been intercepting messages in your bridgework. And just what have you heard people say?"

"Not people. Cops!"

"Okay, cops. What have you heard them say?"

"I've heard them plan different ways they were going to get me. I've heard them talk to my previous lawyers."

"What have they said to your previous lawyers?"

"They've threatened them, talked them out of representing me."

I stared at the man across from me. I wondered if this was the kind of client who would have generated much sympathy from Jenny. He probably would have. I hadn't talked to Jenny in weeks, it occurred to me. I really should call her, I thought. I was sure she was aware that I hadn't been spending as much time with Molly as I should have been. I wondered if she suspected that I was seeing another woman. I wondered if she would have cared. I thought she probably would.

The intercom buzzed.

"There's a Dr. Agroponte on the phone," Sylvia announced. "He says he's the medical examiner."

"He *is* the medical examiner, Sylvia," I said. "Excuse me," I said to Peter, "I have to take this."

I picked up the phone. "Yes, Doctor."

"I completed the re-examination of the body," the doctor said.

"And?"

"There definitely was skin under the nails. What can I say?"

"Then I take it you won't have a problem testifying to that effect?"

"Well, I'm not going to lie about it."

"You'll amend your original autopsy report?"

"Yes, of course. I simply missed it the first time."

"Right."

"There's nothing improper about having my attention called to an oversight by a defense lawyer," the doctor said.

"Right."

"After all, we all make mistakes."

"Of course, Doctor, and I wouldn't want to embarrass you in court about something like that. So you'll be able to say that the skin came from scratches which would indicate a fight?" I was glad I had shown the doctor the color photographs I had insisted Lisa take of the scratches on her stomach. The doctor knew I would have savaged him in court if he denied the connection between the skin under Betz's nails and those scratches.

"Yes, of course."

"You're a man of integrity," I said. I thought he was incompetent, but at least he was willing to admit it, unlike many other expert witnesses who would make every effort to cover up or at least justify their mistakes.

"Thank you," the doctor said.

"Then I'll see you in court. Thank you, Doctor."

I hung up and turned back to Peter. "Okay, Mr. Brown, you hear the cops plotting against you. Have they actually done anything to you?"

"They follow me constantly. They give me tickets for no good reason. They're just trying to wear me down."

"What kind of tickets?"

"They accused me of having a goat in my trunk."

"In your trunk?" I asked, wondering if I was being played with. "In the trunk of your car?"

"You think they open *everybody's* trunk? They planned to get me."

"Are you saying that they actually *found* a goat in your trunk?"

"Cops have no morals."

"You're answering a question I didn't ask," I said, surprised to hear myself sound so impatient. It wasn't simply my eagerness to get back to preparing Lisa's case. This guy was serious, and I was sick of clients like him who drew me into their insane worlds. I used to be intrigued by bizarre stories like this, but now I preferred to sit quietly with Lisa in her apartment and watch videotapes of ballet.

"They don't care about people's rights. I don't know why they should act surprised when someone defends himself."

"Defends himself?" I asked. "How did you defend yourself, Mr. Brown?"

"I shot at them."

"You shot at them? Are you telling me that you shot at the cops after they found a goat in the trunk of your car?"

"You got it."

"Judges usually take shooting at a cop very seriously," I said.

"I know. They were really angry."

"Then how come you're not in jail?"

"I told you. I come from great wealth. My father put up half a million dollars in bail."

"What about these other lawyers? You said that you had other lawyers who are no longer representing you, is that correct, Mr. Brown?"

"I'm not crazy. What would be crazy would be for

me to use insanity as a defense and wind up in a mental institution. I'd spend the rest of my life being fed numbing dosages of Thorazine."

"You're right about that," I said. I looked at the wall behind where my new client was sitting. Bear had sent me a letter just before he retired from the bench, and I had framed it and hung it on my wall. The letter contained an excerpt from a speech Oliver Wendell Holmes had given at a dinner in his honor. Bear had read that speech to me on several occasions when I was clerking for him.

"They were nuts to talk to me about an insanity defense," Peter Brown said.

I got up from my desk and walked over to the framed letter. Peter Brown sat in his chair watching me as I silently read:

I have to ask myself, what is there to show for this half lifetime that has passed? I look into my book in which I keep a docket of the decisions of the full court which fall to me to write, and find about a thousand cases. A thousand cases, many of them trifling or transitory matters, to represent nearly half a lifetime!

Alas, gentlemen, that is life. I often imagine Shakespeare summing himself up and thinking: "Yes, I have written five thousand lines of gold and a good deal of padding—I would have covered the Milky Way with words that outshone the stars!" We cannot live our dreams. We are lucky if we can give a sample of our best, and if in our hearts we can feel that it has been nobly done.

I wondered if Bear had sent me Holmes's words to read when I was dealing with clients like Peter Brown.

I returned to my desk and focused on my new client. "Well, it's clear you're in a pickle, Mr. Brown. I'm in the middle of preparing for a murder case," I said.

"I know. I want you to take my case, Mr. Roehmer. I know you wouldn't let them push me around. I can't believe all this is happening to me. I'm starting to think of myself as a victim," he said. "All of a sudden I feel like people are treating me like I'm an outsider and they have normal lives."

I felt a flash of irony as I recalled how, three months before, I had been whining to Jenny about how tired I was of feeling like an outsider. It was only recently, since I'd been with Lisa, that I had stopped seeing myself as an observer for the first time. Our love was passionate, with an immediacy and spontaneity that I had never experienced before.

I was staring at the man across from me when the intercom buzzed again, bringing me out of my trance.

"Miss Altman is on the line," Sylvia said.

I picked up the phone. "Lisa?"

"Yes, Michael?"

"I have to talk to you. I'm supposed to be starting a trial tomorrow, though there's a remote chance of a plea. If there's a plea, I'll call you in the morning. Otherwise, can you meet me in Judge Taylor's courtroom in the old courthouse at around two?" I wanted Lisa to see my cross-examination in that case so she could be prepared for that kind of attack, which would be different from what I had subjected her to when I had been defending Betz. And I also just wanted to see her.

"I'll be there," she said.

I hung up.

"Aren't we busy," Peter said.

"I've been busier."

"Do you get off on hearing stories like mine?"

"Would you ask a proctologist what drew him to his work?"

"I might, but I was always more curious about criminal lawyers."

I nodded. At the moment I wasn't curious about anything.

"I heard that criminal lawyers were voyeurs. What do you think?" he asked.

"I think I need a few days to decide if this is the kind of case I want to take on," I said, not wanting to prolong the repartee. "I'll be in touch."

"Why do you seem so testy?"

I stood. "I'm sorry. I guess I'm tired."

"When I came here, I was afraid you would have prejudices against me."

"Listen, I don't give a damn if you hear voices or shoot at cops. I'm just preoccupied with a murder case I'm working on. Call it a midlife crisis. Understand?"

Peter nodded.

"I'm sorry. I'm sure you've gone through a difficult time. I'll call you," I said.

An image flashed through my mind of my father. He had worked hard all his life to bring up a son and provide him with an education so that he could use his skills to protect people's rights. Something was wrong. I imagined my father telling me, with that sly smile evident only in his eyes, that his efforts had been intended for a different kind of case than Peter Brown's.

"If I take your case, I will require a retainer of five thousand dollars, payable in advance, before I will start working on it. I will bill you on an hourly basis. My rate is three hundred dollars an hour. If my time uses up your retainer, I will bill you for the difference. If I haven't used up the retainer, I'll return the difference. Understand?"

"That's pretty steep," he said.

"I'm afraid so," I said, and stood up from my desk. "Okay. I'll be speaking to you one way or another in the next few days." Peter got up from his chair and left my office.

I shook my head as I returned to my desk. It had been a long time since I'd found the bizarre world of my clients fascinating.

Maybe Peter Brown was onto something, with his overheard description of lawyers as voyeurs. I had to confess I had sometimes felt thrilled by the exploits of these people who were so unfettered by the normal restraints. They were living dangerously, or crazily, and that was exciting. But I didn't think I was as titillated by the stories as I used to be.

As I sat at my desk I decided then and there that my time handling criminal cases was drawing to a close. I had thought that my decision to turn down Williams, the child-killer, had meant that I would no longer take on monsters as clients. But there was a new problem. This nut that had just been sitting across from me was no monster, just a pathetic victim himself, a mother's son like the rest of humanity. And I still didn't want to have anything to do with him—or his goat.

The difference in my attitudes toward Peter Brown and Lisa stemmed from the fact that I simply didn't have the emotional concern to find out more about Peter. Still, I felt that the way I had treated this mental case had not been professional. Perhaps, I thought, a person eventually loses interest in understanding.

Maybe Lisa's trial would be my last, but before I could get to that I would have to dispose of my gay client's charge of attempted murder. I knew what I had to do there, and I dreaded it. I wondered what Lisa would think of my performance the next day.

Chapter 16

THE FOLLOWING MORNING I was at the kitchen table having coffee while Judith served breakfast to Molly.

Judith was a handsome woman in her early thirties. She kept her coarse black hair cut short and parted mannishly on one side. Her dark eyes were set deep in their sockets and her square chin gave her a determined look. Jenny had interviewed her months before Molly was born, and Judith had become part of our family on the day I brought Jenny and Molly home from the hospital.

"How come Daddy doesn't have to eat lumpy oatmeal?" Molly asked, pointing her spoon at me.

Judith shook her head. "Because daddies have some privileges."

"I wish that were true," I said.

"And don't point your spoon at your father," Judith said.

"Daddy, what does it mean to have a judge of one's pears?" Molly asked.

"I think you mean 'peers,' sweetheart," I said.

"Is it true that even bad people don't have to go to jail if they have a good lawyer?" Molly asked, ignoring my answer.

"Where did you hear that, Molly?"

"Elliot said that."

"Who's Elliot?"

"Elliot's in my play group."

"Elliot may be right," I said. "You know, sweetheart, I miss reading to you at night." I didn't think it appropriate to ask Molly for extra credit for rushing home many mornings from Lisa's apartment at six, as I had done this morning, in order to have a few moments of breakfast with her.

"That's okay. Judith has been reading to me."

"I know. That's fine for you, but *I* miss it. This case that I've been working on has been taking up most of my time. I have to look up a lot of things in books."

"That's okay, Daddy."

"The trial's coming up soon, and once that's over I'll be able to spend more time with you."

A moment later Molly announced that she was sick of oatmeal, and left the table to go to her room to finish the jigsaw puzzle she had started the night before.

"I miss my reading time with Molly," I said to Judith, who was cleaning up the table.

"I'm sure you do. I imagine it's a question of priorities, isn't it?" Judith said, trying, I'm sure, to sound sincere, although I detected a bit of criticism in her voice.

• • •

Later that morning I made my way to the court-house. I pulled hard on the heavy glass door. A crowd of jurors was waiting for the elevators halfway down the main corridor. But just inside the building, a few steps into the corridor on the right, was an unmarked green door of solid steel. I had been behind that door many times, and I knew only too well what to expect.

I opened the door and walked twenty feet down a narrow, windowless, well-lighted hallway to the end, where another green steel door faced me, this one with a perforated, eight-inch in diameter, silver disk in the center. On the wall to the right of the door was a small speaker, and below that a button.

I had waited at that door many times to visit clients who had been unable to come up with enough bail money and were brought over from the jail to start their trials. The last time I had been there was to see Marcus Johnson, my last client before William Betz. Some client! Johnson had poked out the eyes of his rape/robbery victim when he had finished with her to keep her from identifying him. And I had succeeded in getting the case thrown out. Some lawyer!

I sighed and pushed the button, setting off a loud ring, like the fire alarm at my grammar school, only much louder. I released the button and the irritating noise stopped.

"Yeah," a gravelly voice said through the speaker above the button.

"I'm here to see my client."

"Who's your client?" the voice asked.

"Jack Larsen."

"Who are you?"

"Michael Roehmer."

"Hold on." After a pause the voice asked, "Attempted murder? Who's it before?"

"Taylor."

"Taylor?"

"You got it," I said.

"Give me a minute," the voice said.

I waited, as I always did, alone in that corridor, in front of the steel door with that silver-disk eye staring at me. There wasn't a doubt in my mind that my client was not going to take a plea, but I had to ask him. It was probably the last time that he could make the decision, and the decision would have to be his. He'd be the one to do the time if we went to trial and the jury convicted him.

At some point soon I'd have to have a similar conversation with Lisa. It seemed out of the question that the prosecutor could offer Lisa a plea bargain guaranteeing that she wouldn't go to prison—and I didn't think that Lisa would accept a plea even with that guarantee. It would have been impossible for her to say she was guilty when she wasn't.

A buzz at the door startled me. I turned the handle and entered. A few steps in front of me was another solid green door. To the left was a door whose upper half was glass. I opened it and entered the empty lawyers' conference room.

A row of carrels, each with a low, metal stool painted a shiny beige, lined the room. Thick glass walls were in front of each of the carrels. A similar row of carrels was on the other side—the prisoners' side—of the glass walls. I sat on one of the stools and waited.

A few minutes later a guard brought Jack Larsen into the room on the prisoners' side of the glass. Larsen was the only person on that side. He took the seat facing me. We picked up the telephones in front of us.

"How're you doing?" I asked through the telephone.

"I'm okay," Larsen answered.

We stared into each other's eyes through the glass that separated us.

"We should get started this morning," I said.

"They ain't gonna find Perry, are they, Mr. Roehmer?"

"Careful." I pointed to the phone. "I don't trust these things."

"And you're gonna destroy that faggot, Bruce, right?" Larsen asked.

"I'll go as far as Judge Taylor lets me. What you've got to understand is that after we start the trial, the judge won't give his approval to the same deal."

"No deals. I can't. You're gonna destroy that faggot, right?"

"I'm going to try, but there's no guarantee I'll succeed. That's why I want to make sure you realize that if you're convicted, Taylor could give you up to fifteen years, and he's a tough nut who'd probably give you the full fifteen. If you take the plea, you'll walk in three, maybe less."

"Three years is a lifetime."

"A plea to atrocious assault and battery would give you much less time than a conviction for attempted murder."

"If they send me down to Rahway, I won't survive. It'd be a death sentence."

"I understand." I immediately thought of Lisa. God knew what would be done to her if she ever had to spend time with the hardened criminals in the women's prison. The stories were terrifying.

"Bruce has friends down there," he said.

"I know."

Jack Larsen paused. He shook his head. "I'd be raped the day I arrived."

"I'll do the best I can."

"That faggot had it coming, right?"

"I'll tell the prosecutor to forget it."

"Right. Forget it."

We sat quietly for a moment. Jack had paid me $25,000 to represent him. I had no idea where he had gotten the money, and I certainly never asked him. I was quite sure he hadn't gotten it from his job handing out towels at a health club or via a genius grant from the MacArthur Foundation.

"I'll see you upstairs. We'll start your case right away," I said.

"I can't stand the waiting. It's going to make me crazy."

"I know."

Jack Larsen nodded.

We hung up the phones. I watched as Larsen stood up and walked toward his cell.

We picked a jury in less than an hour, and the direct examination of the victim went quickly as well. The victim simply described how my client had attacked him. Then it was my turn on the cross. It was a little after two and Lisa had not yet arrived.

I stood at counsel table next to Jack Larsen, who was seated. Cheryl Hazelton was in her chair at the prosecutor's end of counsel table. The jury was in the box. Bruce Snelling, in his late twenties, dressed in a gray suit and a purple sweater, was on the witness stand.

Just as I was about to begin, I turned around and saw Lisa enter the courtroom. I nodded at her, and she nodded back. I waited for her to take her seat in the back with the other spectators.

I returned to the witness. "Mr. Snelling, are you telling this jury that you did nothing to provoke my client?" I asked, sounding incredulous. "He just chased you around the bedroom that the two of you shared, for no reason, with a twelve-inch bread knife?"

"Yes, sir," Bruce said. He was a handsome young man, with a carefully groomed mustache and goatee. His black skin seemed to have a hue of blue.

"Was this typical of the bedroom behavior the two of you engaged in?" I asked.

"No, sir."

"Do you know where Mr. Larsen got the bread knife?"

"From the kitchen. Perry Lanier saw him take it."

"Yes, we already heard you say that your friend was in the kitchen when my client supposedly grabbed a murder weapon and chased you around the bedroom. But, of course, we haven't heard your friend testify under oath about that, have we?"

Cheryl jumped to her feet. "Objection, Your Honor."

Judge Taylor looked up. "I'll sustain the objection."

"Mr. Snelling, when you say Mr. Larsen suddenly came into the bedroom," I continued, "did you do anything to get away from this knife you say he was brandishing?"

"Of course," Bruce said. "I tried to run away. I kept backing away from him. I kept pleading with him to leave me alone."

"You don't claim that he had ever chased you with a knife before, do you?"

"No, sir."

"Did it occur to you to ask him why this night was different from any other?"

"What do you mean?"

"I mean did you ask him why on this particular night he saw fit to chase you with a twelve-inch bread knife?"

"No, sir."

"Weren't you in the least bit curious?"

"I was too scared to ask him any questions."

"Isn't it a fact, Mr. Snelling, that earlier that evening there had been a large party at your apartment?"

"Yes, sir."

"And didn't you take large amounts of speed at that party?"

"That's just not true."

"Do you have any explanation, then, as to why the hospital that treated you for your wound reported that a large amount of speed was found in your system?"

"No, sir. I may have taken a little of it."

"You may have taken a little bit. I see."

Two of the jurors nodded. They had obviously gotten it.

I turned to Judge Taylor. "Your Honor, may I have a few moments?"

"Certainly," the judge said.

I pushed open the low swinging doors and walked to the rear of the courtroom to where Lisa was sitting.

"You think I was cruel to *you* when I had you on the witness stand?" I whispered to Lisa. "Wait till you see what I have to do now to *this* pathetic soul."

"I know what's required of you," Lisa said. "And I know what you're capable of."

"The point is you have to be ready for this kind of assault," I said.

"I will be," she said, and smiled. I wasn't sure why she smiled. I assumed it was to show me she was confident. Part of me suspected that she was enjoying my performance, and I found that thought a little chilling. Maybe I enjoyed the prospect of showing her how cruel I could be, but that thought didn't occur to me until much later.

I walked back to the well of the courtroom.

"Mr. Snelling, may I ask you to step down from the witness stand and come out here in front of the jury?"

Bruce stood and moved to the spot where I, his cross-examiner, was pointing. I figured the jury would regard him and his walk as effeminate, and have a negative reaction. My client, as luck would have it, walked like a boxer.

"Now, Mr. Snelling, please imagine that I am Mr.

Larsen. Could you demonstrate to the jury how you say you tried to run away from the defendant when he was supposedly chasing you?"

"Certainly. Well, if that were the front door to the bedroom . . ." Bruce pointed to the court stenographer. "I saw him come in the door, and I immediately jumped off of the bed on the side farthest from me." Bruce took a step back. "He came around the bed, and I jumped on top of the bed." Bruce jumped, flapping his arms, bending his knees, as if landing on a raised bed. "I got to the other side. I ran around the bed, and I jumped on the bed to get back to the other side. We went back and forth like that a few times."

As he re-enacted his flight from my client, moving frantically back and forth, Bruce Snelling looked like a hysterical bird. Some members of the jury began to smile. Judge Taylor was staring at the performance; he knew what I was doing and he was angry that I was making the witness look foolish, but he also knew he was helpless to do anything to stop it.

"Then what happened?" I asked.

"He finally caught me."

"Then what happened?" I asked.

"He cut me."

Bruce looked at the jury. And he finally realized that he'd been made to look foolish.

I walked back to my place at counsel table. I looked up at the witness, then focused on the yellow legal pad in front of me. I had written "80 sutures." I picked up the pencil next to the pad. I drew a line through the "80 sutures."

I turned around, checking to confirm that in the

rear of the courtroom Lisa had seen what I had done to the witness.

Slowly, knowingly, she nodded at me.

About twenty minutes later I was standing with Lisa in the corridor outside the courtroom. I explained to her that summations would be made the next day, and that, after instructions from the judge, the jury would decide the case.

"Was there nothing that the judge could do to stop you, Michael?" Lisa asked, conscious of how brutally I had treated the witness.

"I thought he was going to explode," I said, "but there really wasn't anything he could do."

"We should go for a walk," she said.

"Sounds like a good idea," I said. "I think it was good that you saw it."

"Yes, I'm glad I did," she said.

"You have to be prepared for that kind of attack."

"You reminded me of how frightening you can be," Lisa said. "And I'm embarrassed to tell you how sexy you were."

"Sexy?" I said.

"You were wonderful. It felt almost as if I were back on that witness stand with you cross-examining me. You took my breath away then, and you did it again today."

Lisa and I descended a flight of stairs to the second floor and headed toward the large marble staircase that would take us down to the front door.

"Michael," Lisa said, stopping to look directly at me, "I wonder if you realize how powerful you are in the courtroom."

I stared at her lovely, open face with those large, adoring eyes. I didn't know what to say. Slightly embarrassed, all I could do was smile.

She wrapped both her hands around my arm and held it close to her body. We started walking again.

"That's where I clerked my first year out of law school," I said, pointing to a door at the end of the corridor. "It was Bear's courtroom."

"You told me about him. He was the judge you worked for?"

"Right."

"The one who died recently?"

"Right. Would you like to see the courtroom? It's not being used now." They hadn't yet appointed a new judge to replace Bear.

"I'd love to see it," Lisa said.

The courtroom was empty. The room itself was a handsome, wood-paneled space.

Lisa and I walked down the center aisle to the first row of the spectator seats. The room was as quiet as a church. We sat down.

"This is where I started out," I said. At the back of the courtroom, behind the judge's bench, was a door leading to the chambers. The other door at the far end of the courtroom led to what used to be my office over twenty years ago.

Gently Lisa ran the palm of her hand down the side of my face. She knew that this room had a special meaning for me, like no other.

"I keep asking myself how someone could be so astute, so insightful about other people's actions," I said, "and at the same time so stupid, so careless about his own behavior."

"Are you talking about yourself?"

"Of course."

"What provoked this, now?"

"I really don't know."

"Does it have anything to do with me?"

I stood and walked around the empty courtroom. "I remember the first time I ever tried a case in this court. How frightened I was to appear before Bear!"

I walked up the two carpeted steps to the long desk that Bear had used. "It's amazing how the years go by. It all seems so long ago."

Lisa walked up to where I stood. She came up behind me as I gazed out at the grand, wood-paneled room.

I turned around and stared into her beautiful face. We kissed, and we kissed again, and then we got down on the carpeted floor under the judge's bench and made love passionately.

Chapter 17

THE LOUD BELL of the timer went off in Lisa's kitchen. Wearing a large oven mitt, I lifted the heavy cover of a big pot on top of the stove and watched the steam escape from the lamb with juniper berries. I took a bottle of wine from the wine rack on the counter and removed the cork with a "pop."

"Something smells terrific," Lisa said as she entered.

"I think it's going to be okay. Are you hungry?" I asked.

"Ravenous."

"Let me just slice up the meat."

"It's been so long since anyone cooked for me."

"No big deal. I just felt a sudden urge to do something with my hands."

"Am I impressed! Not only is the guy a great lawyer, but he cooks, too."

We both laughed.

A few minutes later, Lisa and I were seated at the table, eating the lamb and drinking the wine. In the dozens of times we'd been together in her apartment over the previous months, we had never talked about the fact that this was the place where my former client had raped her. Lisa had had the grace not to bring it up, and I certainly had never mentioned it. But there hadn't been a single time I'd been there when I hadn't looked around and remembered the scene described at the trial.

"Michael, why aren't you and Jenny still together?" Lisa asked.

"Because of many of the traits that help me to win so many cases," I said. "Maybe I'm just a tad controlling, perhaps a bit suspicious, a touch competitive. That kind of thing," I said, with a forced laugh.

"That can't be true. The way you talk about her, you sound like such good friends."

"She knows I'm struggling with my demons."

"And you both care so much about Molly."

"I don't think it was a coincidence that Jenny's thesis in college was about hero worship in Victorian literature."

"Is that why she fell in love with you? You were some kind of fantasy hero to her?" Lisa asked.

"If I was, I'm sure I've disabused her of that bit of folly," I said.

"If you were, it must have served *both* your needs."

"I suppose you're right," I said.

"Then why did it *stop* serving them?"

I leaned across the table and kissed Lisa. "I'm actually uncomfortable talking about Jenny," I said.

"I respect that."

Lisa took a few sips of the wine.

"Well, if it's any comfort to you," she said, "I want you to know that I don't have any illusions about you."

"That is a comfort." I took a sip of wine. "Do you miss your performances?" I asked. Lisa had taken a leave of absence from her company when the indictment had begun to draw a lot of negative publicity.

"Of course. I'm desperate to get back. Working out every day isn't at all the same as being in front of an audience."

There was a moment of silence.

Lisa held up her glass of wine. "It's good wine, isn't it?" Lisa said.

"Terrific."

"That was quite a job you did on that guy in court today," Lisa said.

"I know," I said.

"But you did what you had to do."

"That was the last time. I can't stand it anymore."

"What do you mean?"

"I can't do this anymore. Not for people I can't stand."

"Well, is this some monumental life decision?"

"I guess so," I said. "No more 'hugger-muggers,' as Jenny used to call them."

"Sounds healthy," Lisa said.

We clinked our glasses in a toast.

As I drank my wine, I studied Lisa. I had always maintained a real distance from my clients. I had taken for granted the common wisdom that getting too close to them would interfere with my judgment. I knew I was already too involved with Lisa to be objective—and above all else, a criminal lawyer needed to be objective.

I wondered if the added pressure I felt to win Lisa's case was going to make it harder for me to make decisions during the trial. There was no question that winning for her was the most important thing in the world to me. I was sure I loved this woman who sat across from me. And I was damn sure I wanted to keep her out of prison.

I was convinced that Lisa didn't have a clue about who I really was, however much she might have thought she did. It had always been difficult for me to reveal any personal truths about myself. Jenny understood me because she had lived with me for so many years. And it was probably because she understood me so well that she left me. It was so much easier for me to interrogate a stranger under oath about the most intimate details of his or her life than to talk about myself in a way that left me exposed even to the slightest degree.

It was not that I was concealing any dark and terrible secrets. In fact, I thought now, there didn't seem to be anything in my early years to suggest the tough, cutoff person I would become. No, that couldn't be true, I realized suddenly—there must be memories that would provide clues . . . vague memories, hidden, I was sure, behind many fine lace curtains. I knew that at some point I would have to try to draw the curtains back.

"My parents used to talk of a lawyer as a power

broker," I said to Lisa, "someone who knew the rules and the players; he could make contacts, get things done—he would have the education and, even more important, the credentials."

My parents were painfully self-conscious about being poor. Their poverty was more than just the absence of money. It made them feel doomed to be outsiders forever, powerless, at the mercy of hostile forces and malevolent people. The idea of their son as a lawyer literally meant having someone who could speak for them, who could assert their rights and protect them from being victims of events over which they had no control. For my parents, "the law" implied a rational order in the world, and the lawyer was the person who upheld that so desperately needed order.

"My mother was photographed when she was seventeen. Her hair was cut short in a boyish style and she wore no makeup. She was dressed in a simple white blouse and black skirt. She sat stiffly with her hands clasped together on her lap, staring into the camera, her dark eyes opened wide. But the eyes looked frightened, almost as if she were waiting for something or someone to slap her. I used to carry that picture around with me in my wallet."

"May I see it?" Lisa asked.

"I must have lost it," I said.

Chapter 18

LATER THAT NIGHT, Lisa and I were in bed. We had made love. The blankets covered us. I was smoking. This was the bed that William had thrown Lisa on, the bed on which he had raped her.

"What are you thinking about?" Lisa asked.

"The medical examiner confirmed that there was skin under William's nails," I said.

"You sound surprised."

"Relieved. Not because I didn't believe you, but because these guys are often incompetent."

"Now that they have this information, why don't they drop the case?"

"The prosecutor's under pressure. Look at all the press this case has gotten." The tabloids had had Lisa's picture on the front page at least a half dozen times, with headlines that should have been reserved for the outbreak of World War III.

"The press has made a big deal out of me, but that's not my fault," Lisa said.

"Of course not, but the prosecutor doesn't want to take responsibility for dismissing it. It's easier for him to let the jury decide. I'm sure he thinks some people on a jury could decide that you killed Betz out of revenge."

"Do you?" Lisa asked.

"No."

"It wasn't revenge, Michael. I swear it."

I nodded.

Lisa leaned over and kissed me. And then we made love again.

"The hardest part of the trial will be in dealing with the fact that you went to his apartment—and with a gun," I said sometime later. We were still in bed.

"But I brought it to his apartment in order to protect myself," Lisa said.

"Of course. But if he had come to your apartment, you could have refused to let him in, or threatened him with your gun without killing him."

"That's true."

" 'That's true' isn't good enough. The prosecutor is going to rip into you on this. You saw what I did to that victim in court today."

"I was so frightened. I just wasn't thinking?"

I nodded. "That's better. You were terrified."

"Right," Lisa said.

"You knew you couldn't call the police about the threats because you were sure they wouldn't believe you. Right?"

"Yes."

I took a deep pull on my cigarette. I knew only too well that some criminal lawyers told a client what to testify to, even when they knew the testimony was untrue. (Although "preparing a witness" in that way is unethical, disbarment rarely results because neither client nor lawyer is likely to tell, and usually there is no other witness to such conversations.) On the other hand, as a lawyer I had the obligation to explain to the client the implications of her testimony, and help her phrase it in a way that would be most impressive to a jury. Of course, I knew there was a thin line between doing that and prompting perjury.

"When you got to his apartment and he threatened to harm you if you didn't have sex with him . . . ?" I probed.

"I was in a state of panic."

"Exactly. And it was only when he started toward you that you grabbed the gun out of your pocketbook and pointed it at him."

"That's right," Lisa said.

"You squeezed the trigger again and again, you don't know how many times, until you stopped pulling the trigger."

"Yes. Yes."

"Then when did you get your scratches?" I asked.

"What?"

"The scratches on your stomach. The strongest evidence we have of your innocence is the scratches on your stomach. If you shot him when he first came after you, when could you have gotten your scratches?"

"Of course. You confused me. He walked toward me, then he lunged and ripped my clothes. That's when he scratched me. I backed away. And when he came at me again, that's when I shot him."

"Better. Lisa, you can't get rattled and forget something like that. The scratches are crucial."

"I understand," she said.

I lit up another cigarette.

"How do you think we'll do?" Lisa asked.

"It depends on the jury. If they believe you, we'll win. If they don't, well, we'll see. I think it's credible."

"At least I won't have *you* cross-examining me in this trial."

"John is a tough lawyer," I said. "Don't underestimate him."

"Does he really think I planned to kill him?"

"I think he believes you were raped last time. He probably doesn't know what really went on when you shot Betz."

"I don't get it. If he has his own doubts, then why would he be trying to convince a jury to convict me of murder?" Lisa asked.

"He's just doing his job."

"I don't know how you people do it. Don't you believe *anybody*?"

"He gave you a break on the bail. But that doesn't mean he won't press hard for a conviction. You have to be ready for a tough cross-examination."

"Is there anything I should do differently from what I did in the last trial?"

"Yes. We'll go through it. You'll be ready by the time we get to court."

"I don't know what I would have done if you hadn't agreed to represent me," Lisa said.

"It'll all depend on our getting the right jury, and how the judge lets me try the case."

"Do we know which judge we'll have?"

"Yes. Grosso."

"What's he like?"

"I've never tried a case with him. He's only been on the bench a year. I hear he's a twerp."

"Well, that's frightening."

"If we play our cards right, I'm sure we can get him on our side."

"When do we go to trial?" Lisa asked.

"After I finish a drug case. Then we'll go. It won't take long."

"I feel so safe in your hands."

I smiled. "Let's go through it again."

"What happens to us after the trial?" Lisa asked. "I mean assuming that I'm acquitted."

"Let's take one step at a time," I said, although that was a question I had already asked myself dozens of times. At this point I only knew that I desperately wanted to win the case for Lisa. I was sure she was innocent, and I was sure I was in love with her. And I was also convinced that more was riding on this case, both personally and professionally, than on any other in my career. And I couldn't bear to contemplate the consequences of a conviction.

Chapter 19

THE NEXT MORNING I woke up and realized I was next to Lisa, in her bed, in her apartment. The clock on the table next to me said 7:30. I had spent dozens of nights at her apartment, but I was still almost always disoriented when I woke up.

I picked up the phone and dialed home.

"Hello," Judith said in her British accent.

"Judith?" I said.

"Good morning, Michael." There was a touch of disapproval in Judith's voice, but I felt I had it coming.

"Something came up, so I couldn't get home last night. How's Molly?" I had been making this kind of early-morning call about twice a week lately, and I was feeling guilty about it.

"Molly's fine. We're about to go off to nursery."

"Okay. I just wanted to check in. I'll see you later.

I'll be home to change and then I have to be in court. Tell Molly I'll see her tonight."

I was in the courthouse two hours later to file a motion to compel the state to give better medical treatment to Sherry Parruco, the client of mine who had not used enough lighter fluid to burn her boyfriend. Sherry was doing her time in the women's prison. She had been diagnosed as a diabetic when she'd gone into insulin shock soon after arriving there, but the officials at the prison hospital, out of spite or incompetence, had not been giving her the medication she needed.

After dropping off the motion papers at the clerk's office, I headed to the cafeteria. I was still troubled by the thought that I had secured Larsen's acquittal by making a direct appeal to the jury's prejudices against gays. What I had done was immoral—there was no way of getting around that. Maybe it was within the guidelines of ethical conduct for a lawyer, but I knew it was personally immoral. And that had been a case in which I hadn't cared about my client in any personal way. It frightened me to think of what I would be willing to do to win Lisa's case.

I was also worried about whether or not I would be able to conduct Lisa's trial with that same kind of professional detachment that was needed to be effective. I knew I'd never forgive myself if I lost my temper. The irony was how successful my professional detachment had made me against Lisa when I was defending Betz. Look what my skill had put Lisa through as a result of that win!

I opened the door and stepped onto the small stage

of a platform which looked down on the enormous room that was the cafeteria. At tables scattered about were a flock of court attendants, a whisper of witnesses, a plague of lawyers, an infestation of people suing people, and a fistful of people accused of crimes. In the far corner by the window, I noticed a woman and four men seated around a rectangular table: a pride of judges—Leonard Grosso, Dick Bennett, Lois Shearer, Tony Fazio, and Andrew Taylor.

I descended the stairs and moved to my left, pushing through the turnstile. I poured coffee into a plastic foam cup and walked over to Lucille, the woman at the cash register. In her mid-sixties, Lucille had worked in the courthouse cafeteria at least since the time I'd clerked for Bear. She was an eccentric, feisty pistol who terrified most people with whom she came in contact.

"Good morning, Lucille," I said, handing her some money.

"Yeah. Good morning," she responded snappishly, ringing up the register.

"Well, you seem particularly chipper today," I said.

"I learned to fake it in charm school. Did you get any more bums off today, Counselor?"

"Lord knows, I try, every day, in every way," I said.

"Everybody still a potential client?" she asked.

"Seems that way," I said, smiling at the running joke we shared. I took my change and moved on.

I made my way to a table near the judges where three of my friends—Darren Gallagher, Norman Dogbein, and Ashley Josephs—were sitting. I lowered myself into an orange plastic chair.

"Gentlemen," I said, nodding at my friends.

My friends nodded back.

Darren Gallagher and I had been in the same class in law school. Although we had never been close, we had worked together, some twenty years before, setting up a student civil rights organization. I had always found Darren to be a bit self-righteous and an opportunist. I couldn't fault him for being ambitious, not without feeling like a hypocrite myself, but his self-righteousness sometimes got on my nerves. He was the chief trial lawyer for Legal Aid, but he introduced himself to strangers as a movement lawyer, which was ridiculous. His criminals were like everybody else's, only poorer.

The judges were less than twenty feet away. Darren was staring at Leonard Grosso, the judge with whom I would be spending the next few weeks trying Lisa's case. Grosso was dressed in a tight-fitting, double-breasted suit with wide lapels and pronounced shoulder pads.

"So when he's being led out," I could overhear Grosso say, "the guy calls to me, 'You know, Judge, for such a little guy you give really big time.'" Grosso, his coarse black hair combed straight back, laughed louder than the other judges at the table. Darren Gallagher, at my table, glowered with a mixture of contempt and envy.

"Darren, you look as if you could kill someone," I said.

"You wouldn't believe the way they talk," Darren said.

"Darren's problem," Norman Dogbein said, "is

that he sees judges as father figures, and he feels personally betrayed every time they act like schmucks."

"Look how smug and self-satisfied they are," Darren said.

"You're too harsh," I said. "For most of them it's a kind of semi-retirement, just a gavel at the end of the rainbow." I knew I was sounding generous, although I usually had as much anger toward judges as Darren.

"They go nuts once they get their robes," Ashley Josephs said. Josephs was young, barely thirty, with eyebrows that seemed to meet to form one long line. We had tried a drug case together several years before. Our clients had been young ghetto kids charged with possessing a kilo of marijuana with the intent of selling it. The cops had found the evidence in my client's apartment. It was Ashley's first trial, and he'd been frightened. We'd gone through the whole trial together, and as we'd waited for the verdict, Ashley had gotten more nervous. He couldn't stand the prospect that his client would be convicted. The prosecutor had offered both our clients a plea to mere possession, and as the jury was deliberating, Ashley talked his client into taking it. About an hour later the jury brought back a verdict of not guilty of all charges against my client. Had he waited that extra hour his client would almost surely have been acquitted too. Ashley and I both remembered that plea whenever we got together.

"I was in court when Grosso was still a defense lawyer like us," Norman said. "He was defending this beautiful woman accused of killing her husband. He was in the middle of his summation, standing in front of the jury. Suddenly he points at his client and with intense seriousness says, 'I ask you, ladies and gentlemen of the jury, are these the legs of a murderess?'"

Everyone at the table laughed.

"Michael, you missed hearing Norman tell us yet again about his first case," Ashley said.

"Not again, Norman," I said. "Have you no sense of decency?"

"I gave you *your* first case, you ungrateful whore," Norman said.

"How can I forget it? Haven't I thanked you recently?" I asked. "The creep could have gotten life. He owed me two-thirds of the fee, and I never saw him again. Thanks a lot, Norman."

"You knew you wouldn't get the money," Norman said. "You wanted the case. Tell the truth."

"Maybe so," I said. "You learn."

"You learn that if you're a criminal lawyer, you're working for criminals," Norman said, as he so often did.

"I know: Mother Teresa doesn't need a criminal lawyer," I said, which Norman also said quite often.

"Right. If I've told you once, I've told you a hundred times," Norman said.

John Phalen, carrying a cup of coffee, arrived at our table. "Mind if I join you?" John asked as he placed his cup across from me and sat down.

"Careful, everybody. It's the virile fist of the state," Norman said.

"Oh, Michael, congratulations on the Larsen case," John said.

"Thanks. One of my prouder moments," I said sarcastically.

"Another win, Michael?" Norman asked. "And you haven't told us about it?"

"I'd just as soon forget it," I said.

"Michael's client puts a twelve-inch bread knife into the stomach of his male lover. Leaves him with a million stitches. And Michael gets his man off," Ashley said.

"What was your defense, Michael?" Norman asked. "That he mistook the victim for a challah?"

"That's not bad, Norman: the old challah defense," Ashley said.

"My guy's gay, right?" I said. "He's the victim's lover, for Christ's sake, and he keeps calling the victim a faggot."

"It was a nice win," John said.

"I made a blatant appeal to the jurors' prejudices against gays," I said.

"I heard about it," John said.

"I don't ever want to do something like that again," I said.

Judges Taylor and Grosso arrived at the table.

"And how are our most distinguished members of the criminal bar today?" Judge Taylor asked.

All of us at the table nodded at the two judges, except Darren, who took a sip of coffee and stared at Judge Grosso.

Grosso leaned over the table. "I was just telling my brothers on the bench that the reason Cain didn't get a death sentence for killing his brother wasn't so much that God was against capital punishment as because Cain didn't have a lawyer to muck things up for him." Grosso smiled at what he regarded as good-natured kidding.

"Well, Judge," I said, "I've sometimes wondered how much worse it would have been for all of us if Eve had taken a bite out of a judge instead of the apple."

"Well put," Norman roared.

I had spoken out of reflex, without really thinking that I was about to start a trial with this man and that the last thing I needed was to antagonize him.

"That's good, very good," Judge Grosso said without smiling. "Well, you all have a good day." Grosso walked away, and Taylor followed him.

"Look at him, that little shrimp," Darren said, still staring at Grosso. "They shouldn't make anyone under five-six a judge."

"I wish I'd tried a case against Grosso when he was still a prosecutor," Norman said. "I'd have beaten his ass."

"What do you mean when he *was* a prosecutor? He still acts like a prosecutor," Darren said.

"What have you got going today, Michael?" John asked.

"I was supposed to have an insanity case, but it got postponed."

"We have the Altman case. You're still in on that one, aren't you?"

"Yes. I guess so. Any chance of dismissing it?" I asked, trying not to sound too anxious.

"I already spoke to Grosso about throwing the case out."

"Oh, really?" I was surprised John had not mentioned to me that he intended to speak to Grosso about a dismissal. It was clear to me now that John really didn't want to try the case. "What did Grosso say?" I asked.

"Five bullets."

"That's what he said, 'Five bullets'?"

"What he said was the first was self-defense, the second manslaughter. By the fifth, Grosso said, we're talking first degree, premeditated murder."

"First degree? You can't be looking for first degree!"

"Michael, that's what he said. He thinks the woman is taking us for fools."

"I don't think so," I said.

"I don't know. I don't think Grosso believes any women."

"Great."

"All I want is to move it quickly and get it over with. Grosso's pushing for a quick date," John said.

"Why? What's the rush?"

"He thinks he'll get some press with it," John answered. "I can't believe all the interviews I've turned down on this case."

"What the hell does he need press for?"

"I think he wants to run for public office."

"Really?"

"The rumors are governor."

"Great. There should be a height requirement for governor," I said.

Chapter 20

LATE THAT AFTERNOON I met Jenny at the luncheonette around the corner from my office. She had asked to see me, but wouldn't tell me why. She was waiting at a table when I arrived, dressed in a smart brown silk business suit, her hair cut short and boyishly parted. All in all she looked on top of things, and very serious.

"Michael," she said soon after I sat down, "you know I've never been critical of your relationship with Molly."

I nodded. I knew what was coming.

"I know you love her more than anything in the world," she said. "You'd kill for her, as you would say. And Lord knows, I have my own guilt about not spending enough time with her. But lately I gather you've not been coming home most nights, and, well . . ."

"Jen, you know I have this murder case. It's coming

to trial in the next few days," I said. I had a vivid memory of the argument I'd had with Jenny soon after we'd separated. She had made clear to me that she wouldn't try to work out a reconciliation, but was intent instead on a divorce. I couldn't recall whose temper had exploded first. But I did remember Jenny calling me a self-centered little boy and me calling her a cold, castrating bitch. We'd had this "elevated discussion" in a cheap cafeteria surrounded mostly by homeless people in from the cold. I didn't have the faintest recollection, as I now sat with Jenny in this luncheonette, how we had wound up in that cafeteria then, but I certainly remembered well how all the other patrons stared at us as we shouted at each other. I really didn't want to let the present conversation get out of control.

"It's not fair to Molly," she said. "All of a sudden you're gone. You've never done that before. It's like changing the ground rules."

"Molly seems fine."

Jenny looked into my face intently. "You're sleeping with that woman, aren't you?"

I struggled to think of what to say, but before I could think of an answer, she stood up and left.

Chapter 21

I HELD OPEN the door of the courtroom for Lisa. As we headed down the center aisle of the crowded room, I took a deep breath. I recognized a few of the ever-present fans from earlier trials sitting in their specta-tor seats. John Phalen was already seated at his end of counsel table, the side closest to the jury box.

"Mr. Roehmer," Judge Grosso said, pointing at me as I was about to sit down.

"Good morning, Judge," I said, and remained standing.

"You haven't been in my court before, and I'd like to straighten out a few things at the outset so that we don't have any problems."

"You can sit down, Lisa," I said, pointing to the chair next to me.

"I may be new to the bench but your reputation has preceded you. I want to make it clear that I'm not going to put up with any improper behavior," Judge

Grosso said, looking over at the newspaper reporters arrayed in the first row of the spectator seats. "Do you understand that?"

I placed my briefcase down on the table. "Judge, I've been trying cases for over twenty years, and one thing I've learned is that I shouldn't engage in improper behavior. Lord knows, we all just try to do our job as best we can." My first thought was that this little man in black robes must be out of his mind. The two court officers, the court clerk, and the judge's law secretary were watching me.

"Well, you don't need to get cute with me. I expect you to behave within the bounds of proper decorum. I'm just putting you on notice right up front about that."

"I appreciate the notice, and I will certainly try to restrain the demons inside me," I said, "as I'm sure you will try to do the same." I didn't have to add the last part, but it came out of my mouth before I could catch it.

"I can see we're going to have trouble here. But I can tell you now that I'm not going to be the loser in any contest."

"If Your Honor is going to get emotional about having me in his court, maybe you should excuse yourself from trying this case and transfer it to another judge." I knew there was no way in hell he was going to let this trial slip away from him, not with this audience.

"I will not excuse myself. I was trying to get some guidelines straight. Let's get on with the case."

I sat down at counsel table. I felt like grabbing the

judge's greasy hair with both hands and smashing his face down into his desk. Instead, I smiled.

"A new jury panel is being sworn in this morning, so we'll start picking our jury this afternoon." Grosso banged his gavel and walked down the three steps from his bench and left the courtroom.

"Can we get a different judge?" Lisa whispered to me.

I shook my head. "This trial is going to be a lot harder than I expected," I said.

Chapter 22

As the courtroom emptied out, Lisa said she wanted to go home. I told her I would meet her back in the courtroom later that afternoon. She walked out the door, and I was suddenly alone and seething. Having a judge as an adversary in a trial was a major drawback for a lawyer, and a bad situation for any client. But I had the feeling I was not going to have much luck in getting Grosso on my side. This was just the kind of dilemma that I used to talk to Bear about. He'd always managed to come up with a sensible solution.

I decided that I would have a chat with Dick Bennett, who had been such a good friend of Bear's. Bennett had been the judge in the trial against Betz, so he certainly knew a lot about the case, and he had told me at Bear's funeral that he knew how important Bear had been to me and that he would be happy to talk to me if I ever felt the need for fatherly advice.

The judges in the courthouse took turns swearing in the new jury panels. By coincidence, Bennett would be swearing in the jury panel that would produce the twelve jurors who would decide Lisa's fate. Bennett would give an orientation speech to the new jurors that would set the tone for their two-week encounter with criminal justice. The judge's job was to inspire the jurors to do their duty.

I entered the large room of what was called the jury control room, and took a seat in the back row, the last of twenty rows. In the front of the room was a long counter, and immediately to the right of it was a large American flag. In front of the counter was a lectern, and on the wall behind it was a large clock. It was 10 A.M.

Richard Bennett, dressed in the black robes of his profession, was standing at the lectern in front of the room looking out at the almost two hundred men and women summoned from the community. He must have just been introduced, because he was only now opening the black, three-ringed notebook resting on the lectern.

The room was silent as the random mix of people from the community respectfully, anxiously, waited for the judge to speak. Bennett was to talk about the majesty of the law and the importance of jury service in the American system of justice. He, like the other judges with years of experience on the bench, had delivered his version of the speech dozens of times before. Bear used to enjoy handling this assignment and over the years had done it many times.

"Ladies, gentlemen, members of our community," Bennett began, "from grammar school on we have learned about our rights as Americans, but aside from voting, most of us have had few opportunities to participate actively in the democratic process. In a criminal trial the citizens themselves make fateful decisions in a direct expression of power."

Two court attendants in uniform were standing at the back of the large room, one of them apparently telling the other a joke. A clerk sitting at a desk at the side of the room was chewing gum and filling out forms.

My mind wandered as Judge Bennett took the jurors through the familiar litany. I remembered the day that Bear, in his robes, had sworn me in as a prosecutor. Jenny had held the Bible for me in Bear's chambers. I was so nervous that when I removed my hand from the Holy Book, I left my handprint on the leather.

"If you do your duty as you are instructed," Judge Bennett said, softly, almost to himself, "you will reap the rich reward reserved for those who rise to the call of public service."

I was impressed, as I always was, at the attentive and respectful attitude the jurors showed toward a judge. They were clearly hanging on to Judge Bennett's every word.

Allen Swid sat down next to me. He had written articles on the Betz trial, and he had already written about the case against Lisa. He held a small spiral notebook in one hand and a pen in the other.

I nodded at him.

"I was in the courtroom this morning. It looks like it might be a rough trial for you, Mike," Swid said.

"I *thought* I saw you smiling," I said.

Swid turned to a page in his notebook and read to me. "Of the variety of ways that judges exercise power, none is more immediate or more awesome than their control over lawyers." He put the notebook down and looked at me, waiting for a reaction.

I tried to smile. Someday, I thought, Molly will be just starting out in a career, and might sound as naive as this young man. I shook my head. No, Molly would never be such a jerk.

"I'm working on an article, a feature article, maybe even a cover story for a magazine. It's about judges," Swid said.

"That's very interesting," I said. Allen knew I was being sarcastic.

"It's really amazing how respectful the jurors are to judges, don't you think?"

"Absolutely," I said.

Swid wrote some notes in his little book. He looked up again at me. "Judges, after all, are the critical focus of the justice system, leading the average person through the maze of legal mysteries that ultimately guarantee our constitutional rights. Wouldn't you say?"

"No question about it. I couldn't have said it better."

Swid wrote some more notes in his little book.

"There should be a deep satisfaction," Judge Bennett could be heard saying, "in having borne an important civic responsibility with honor and distinction, regardless of the results."

"How much do you think the jurors really understand what he's talking about?" Swid asked.

"Enough," I said. "Enough to realize it's a serious responsibility they're being asked to take on."

"Well, Mike, do you think Grosso is going to give you a fair trial?"

"You don't really expect me to answer that, do you, Allen?"

"Nope. Just thought I'd try." Swid rose to leave. "I'll see you in court tomorrow."

"Of course."

I tried to catch where Judge Bennett was in his speech. Bennett was looking down at his notebook on the lectern. He had a pained expression on his face.

"Deep satisfaction. There should be deep satisfaction," Judge Bennett said. "Pride . . . I don't . . . Who knew?" He paused and looked down at his notebook. He seemed unable to continue.

I was struck by the silence. Bennett was clearly struggling. Something was wrong.

"I've been a judge now for almost eighteen years," he said. "Eighteen years of criminal trials . . . one atrocity after another . . . an endless parade of monsters doing unspeakable . . . such savagery . . . to fellow human beings . . . You try . . . nothing seems to matter . . . they just keep coming."

The clerk and the court attendants exchanged glances. It had finally occurred to them that something unusual was happening.

I stood and headed toward the lectern.

Judge Bennett began to sob. "The cruelty . . . I had no idea. When I began . . ."

I arrived at Judge Bennett's side and put my arm around his shoulder. "It's all right, Judge," I said.

"The bastards . . ." Judge Bennett said.

"Tell the clerk to swear in the jury," I gently said.

"Swear the jury," Judge Bennett obediently said.

Shaken and confused by what they had just witnessed, the jurors stood for the oath. The clerk walked to the lectern.

"Please raise your right hands," the clerk said.

The jurors obeyed.

"Do you solemnly swear," the clerk read from a dog-eared three-by-five card, "that you will support the Constitution of the United States and the Constitution of this state, so help you God? Please respond 'I do.'"

"I do," the jurors responded.

A court attendant and I led Bennett into a small office, outside the jury control room. I waited with the judge as the attendant called his family to come to the courthouse.

Chapter 23

LATER THAT DAY, an hour into the afternoon session, Judge Grosso was on the bench and fourteen people were in the jury box. The back of the courtroom was filled with the rest of the jury panel. John and I were at our places at counsel table. Lisa was seated next to me.

"If any of you have ever been convicted of a crime, please so indicate by raising your hand," Judge Grosso said to the jurors in the box.

None of the jurors raised a hand.

"Have you or any member of your family ever been the victim of a crime? Please indicate so by raising your hand," Judge Grosso said.

Almost half the jurors in the box raised their hand. "Welcome to urban America," I muttered to myself.

"What?" Lisa asked.

"It's not important," I said.

"Okay. Let's start with Juror Number One. That's you," Judge Grosso said, checking his notes, "Mrs. Rothbart."

"My house was broken into about a year ago. Some things were taken," Mrs. Rothbart said.

"Will that prejudice you in any way against this defendant?" Judge Grosso asked.

"I'll never get over it. I felt so violated."

"Do you think you would hold that experience against the defendant in this case?" Judge Grosso asked.

"No, I don't think so."

"Okay. Juror Number Three. That's you," Judge Grosso said, again consulting his notes, "Mr. Carey."

"My wife's pocketbook was stolen. She was just walking down the street," Mr. Carey said.

"Will that prejudice you in any way against this defendant?" Judge Grosso asked.

"I guess not," Mr. Carey said.

"Guessing is not good enough. Would it or would it not?" Judge Grosso asked.

"No, it would not."

"Juror Number Seven." Judge Grosso checked his notes. "Mrs. Grosstuck."

"Our car was stolen. Does that count?" Mrs. Grosstuck said.

"Of course. Your property was taken," Judge Grosso said. "Do you think that would prejudice you in any way against this defendant?"

"Should it?"

"Of course not. But I'm asking you if it will."

"No, it will not," the woman said.

"Good. Juror Number Eleven." Judge Grosso checked his notes. "Miss Davis."

"Can I speak to Your Honor privately?" Miss Davis asked.

"Yes. Come over here. This is what we call sidebar." Judge Grosso pointed to the side of his desk farthest from the jury. "Counsel and the court reporter, please," Judge Grosso said.

The juror made her way to sidebar, where she was joined by the court reporter, John, and me.

"Yes?" Judge Grosso said to the woman standing next to him.

"Your Honor, I was once raped," Miss Davis said. "It was in college, almost twenty years ago. I was on a date, a blind date, and at the end of the evening he just forced himself on me."

"Miss Davis, this case might involve allegations of rape or attempted rape," Judge Grosso said. "I take it you are saying that that terrible experience would prejudice you in this case. Is that correct?"

"Objection," I said. "Your Honor, you are slanting the questions so as to incline this juror to disqualify herself."

"I am not, Counselor," Judge Grosso said with irritation. "I'll ask the question any way I see fit. When I'm done, you can ask her your question. Miss Davis, please answer me. I take it your experience might affect your decision in this case. Is that correct?"

"I honestly don't know. I'm afraid it might," Miss Davis said.

"Okay, Mr. Roehmer, how would you phrase the question?" Judge Grosso said.

"Miss Davis, you said that that unfortunate incident happened twenty years ago," I said. I knew this juror was going to be excused, but I didn't want the judge to excuse her. I wanted the prosecutor to have to use one of his challenges. "Would that experience still influence your judgment in this case? Would you hold it against this defendant or against the state and therefore be unable to reach a verdict solely on the evidence presented in this case?"

"I guess not," Miss Davis said.

"If you take an oath to decide this case solely on the evidence presented here, you would follow that oath, wouldn't you?" I asked.

"Yes, I would."

"Your Honor, I would object to excusing this juror," I said. "I believe her when she says she would abide by her oath to evaluate this case on its merits, notwithstanding her prior experience."

"I'll excuse this juror. You can return to the jury control room," Judge Grosso said to Miss Davis. "Counsel can return to their places."

Grosso and I glowered at each other for a moment, and then the prosecutor, the court reporter, and I returned to our places.

"If any of you have served as jurors before, please indicate so by raising your hand," Judge Grosso said to the remaining jurors in the box.

Three jurors raised their hand.

"Okay. Would that experience influence your ability to be fair and impartial jurors in this case?" Judge Grosso asked.

The three jurors shook their heads.

"I take it by your silence that the answer is no," Judge Grosso said.

"Your Honor, may we ask what kind of cases these jurors sat on?" I asked.

"All right," Grosso said, and turned to the jurors. "But don't tell us what the verdict was or if there was a hung jury. Juror Number Three?"

"Burglary. It was a burglary."

"Juror Number Five?"

"It was a drug case."

"Juror Number Ten?"

"Mine was also a drug case, but we couldn't reach a verdict," the woman said, apparently unaware that she had ignored the judge's instructions not to reveal if she had been on a hung jury.

"Satisfied, Mr. Roehmer?" Judge Grosso asked.

"Thank you, Judge. You're too kind," I said. Murder cases like this one were much better prepared than cases involving less serious crimes. I knew that jurors who had sat on a less serious charge would be impressed by all the witnesses and scientific evidence in the case they were about to hear against Lisa. If this were a burglary, I'd have been eager to keep a juror who had sat on a murder case, because he'd be seeing much less evidence and far fewer witnesses.

I was determined to excuse everyone but the juror who had been on a hung jury. The prosecutor would excuse her—John wouldn't take the risk that she had been the holdout on that jury. A hung jury would be a loss for the prosecutor. There would probably be a retrial, but if the second trial also resulted in a hung jury, the prosecutor would, I was sure, have to dismiss the charges against Lisa.

"If any of you have heard or read anything about this case, please indicate so by raising your hand," Judge Grosso said. A photograph of Lisa was on the front page of two of the city's tabloids that very day. Betz's trial had received enormous attention, and this trial against Lisa was the climax to that buildup. I had never seen anything like it.

Every single juror in the box raised a hand.

"Okay," Judge Grosso said. "Do any of you who have raised your hand feel that what you have heard or read about the case would prevent you from arriving at a decision in this case solely on the evidence presented at the trial?"

No one raised a hand.

About an hour later I was standing in front of the jury box speaking to the prospective jurors.

"Ladies and gentlemen of the jury," I said, "my client is charged with the most serious crime: murder. The evidence will show that she was the victim in this case, the victim of a nightmare that had gone on for months."

"Mr. Roehmer," Judge Grosso interrupted, "it's a little early for a summation. We're supposed to be picking a jury. If you have a question, ask it."

"Of course, Judge. I was just getting to it." I restrained my anger because I knew I risked alienating the jury if I talked back to the judge. A jury saw a judge as the sole authority in the courtroom, officiating in an unbiased way over the trial, in control of everything that went on throughout the contest. I kept my attention on the jury.

"You will hear testimony about my client's state of mind during the period leading up to the killing and at the critical moment of the shooting," I said. "What I need to ask—and I ask it reluctantly, but it is essential that I do so—is whether any of you have ever had occasion to feel sexually harassed or sexually threatened."

Grosso pounded his gavel. "I'm not going to allow that question," he said. "It would be a terrible invasion of this jury's privacy."

"Your Honor," I said.

"They are not on trial here. It's hard enough to get jurors without subjecting them to improper questions," Grosso said.

"Your Honor, may counsel approach sidebar?" I asked.

"Of course," Judge Grosso answered.

John and I returned to the side of the judge's desk, along with the court reporter, who placed her machine once again on the judge's desk.

"Your Honor," I said, "the testimony regarding the defendant's mental state is crucial to my case. If any of the jurors have felt sexually harassed, that would be important information about the jurors. In order to avoid the chance of embarrassment, perhaps each juror could be questioned privately in your chambers."

"I'm not going to allow such questions in private or in public," Judge Grosso said. "You have no right to invade the privacy of these people."

"But Your Honor, I have a right to determine if they have some preconceived notions about fears of sexual assault."

"Then ask them that, but I won't allow you to put these people on trial here. Their personal histories are private, and should be allowed to remain that way."

"I don't want to put them on trial. I just want a fair trial for my client."

"And I'm here to make sure she gets one. Now let's get on with it."

"If I'm limited to asking only if any of them have any prejudices against people who say they are afraid of being raped, they're simply going to say they don't."

"I've made my ruling. I don't intend to continue arguing with you. Go back to your place, and let's move on."

"Judge, I don't think you're being fair."

"Don't whine. We obviously disagree, but I'm the judge, and I've ruled."

"And so will an appeals court."

"That sounds like a threat, Mr. Roehmer. You, like any lawyer, have a right to appeal, but you don't have the right to threaten me. I'll hold you in contempt if you do it again. Do you understand?"

"Yes, sir."

Judge Grosso was fuming. Judges were usually aware when lawyers were trying to build a record for reversal on appeal, and they usually didn't take it personally. But I had a real adversary in Judge Grosso, and I wasn't doing a very good job of protecting my client from him. Grosso could try to bury Lisa in a variety of ways that would be hard for an appeals court to notice. A cold transcript would not convey the impression of a voice dripping with sarcasm or seething with anger; an appellate judge reading the transcript could easily miss the influence of a skillful judge's manner or tone on the outcome of a trial. I knew things could, and probably would, get worse—a lot worse.

"So what do you think about the jurors?" I asked Lisa about an hour later. The time had come to make some decisions about which people should rule on whether Lisa had planned to kill Betz or whether she had acted out of self-defense.

"I don't like the guy in the third seat," Lisa said.

"Why? He seems fine to me."

"He frightens me. There's something about his eyes that reminds me of him." I knew that by "him" Lisa meant Betz.

"He's an engineer. I like engineers. They measure things as part of their work, and I think they look at 'reasonable doubt' as a wall the prosecutor's got to build."

"Please, Michael. He frightens me."

"Okay. Anyone else?"

"No, I guess not. What do you think?" Lisa asked.

"The kraut in the back. I think her name's Gross-tuck or something. I want to get rid of her."

"The name might be German, but she didn't speak with an accent."

"Lisa, call it a quirk, but my parents fled Europe just before the war. I don't keep Germans on my juries, whether they talk with an accent or not."

"Michael, my father was German."

"Then I wouldn't keep you on one of my juries either."

"Okay. Anyone else?" Lisa asked.

"Look at the way the guy at the end of the first row is looking at you. Look at that smile."

"He just looks nervous to me."

"That's not nerves. Trust me, Lisa."

"I trust you, Michael."

"The guy in the middle, in the back row."

"What's wrong with him? He's got three daughters. I think he'll be protective of women," Lisa said.

"I have a feeling he fools around himself. He'll be protective of men. When he hears the testimony, he won't think abut his daughters being assaulted, he'll probably think of his own reactions to women."

I stood. "Your Honor," I said, "the defense will excuse Jurors Number Three, Five, Seven, and Fourteen." The problem was that I didn't want to be left with an all-woman jury. I was taking a risk on who would be called to replace the jurors I'd just excused.

"Very well," Judge Grosso said. "Call the next jurors. Let's finish this up, gentlemen, and get on with the trial."

As the questioning of the new jurors began, I thought about the choices I had just made. I knew my attitude toward a jury simply reflected my view of people in general. That was the way the system worked. I had to pick juries by making fundamental judgments about human nature on the basis of superficial information; and on those judgments I was betting on the way the particular jurors would respond to my efforts to influence or—more accurately—manipulate them. Looked at this way, my choices of whom to include in or exclude from the jury revealed more about me than about the jurors who would ultimately decide Lisa's fate.

Chapter 24

ON THE AFTERNOON after the jury selection was completed, I was able to keep an appointment at Molly's nursery. Her teacher had written me a note to say that my Molly was having some difficulty with one of the other kids in her class.

When I spoke to the teacher, a Mrs. Talbot, she told me that Molly and a little boy in the class by the name of Kevin were constantly fighting.

"What is it that they are fighting about, Mrs. Talbot?" I asked, trying not to sound hostile.

"Well, it's not the content of the fighting that worries me. It's that it is almost constant. And it's terribly disruptive for the others in the class." Mrs. Talbot nodded at me as if she were hoping that I would understand. I didn't.

"Are you telling me that you don't know what they fight about? Have you asked either of them?"

"Of course. They fight over this and that. Each

fight is over something new. I've spoken to the little boy about hitting girls, and I've repeatedly told Molly that her behavior in fighting back is unbecoming to a young lady. Nothing seems to help."

"Then, the little boy seems to be starting these fights?"

"The boy may be the first to start hitting, but I'm afraid it's because Molly taunts him. That's why I thought it was important to speak to the parents."

"Well, I'm glad you did, Mrs. Talbot. Don't you ever again tell my daughter that defending herself in a fight is unbecoming to a young girl. Do you understand?" I didn't mean to slam my fist on the table I was sitting at, but it certainly caught Mrs. Talbot's attention.

When I saw Molly that night, I told her not to torment this kid anymore.

Chapter 25

"LADIES AND GENTLEMEN, now that you have been selected as jurors," I said, beginning my opening statement, "it is my opportunity to stress to you that you will have to decide this case solely on the basis of the evidence that is introduced during the trial."

I knew that my major threat to an acquittal was going to be the judge. I decided I would have to begin immediately to make the jury believe that Grosso was being unfair. The jury came to court convinced that a judge was an impartial, fair umpire. I knew that was often untrue. Grosso was clearly out for a conviction, and I had to plant seeds in the jurors' minds that this judge was being unfair. This was the trickiest and probably most difficult way to win a case, but I didn't think I had any choice.

"What I or the prosecutor tell you during the course of the trial is not evidence," I said. "And for that matter, *not even something that the judge tells you* is evidence. The judge is supposed to be a fair arbiter of the rules of procedure and the laws you must apply. My client is presumed innocent, and that presumption stays with her throughout the trial. And nothing that the prosecutor says, *nothing even that the judge may say*, alters that fundamental principle. By your oath you have sworn, in effect, not to be bullied by the prosecutor *or by the judge*, but to decide the case fairly on the evidence presented. Thank you."

When I finished, I returned to my seat at counsel table next to Lisa.

"Members of the jury," Judge Grosso said, glancing over to the members of the press in the front row of the spectator seats, "Mr. Roehmer is quite correct when he indicates that *I* run this courtroom. Nothing the lawyers say is evidence. And by your oath you have sworn to accept the law you will apply in this case from me, not from the prosecutor *and not from Mr. Roehmer*."

It was clear to me that I was right in seeing Grosso as an adversary, and he certainly understood what I was trying to do in my opening statement—he knew I had thrown down a gauntlet. His response was his effort to neutralize what I had said. And we both knew he had succeeded.

When a judge pretended to be fair and disinterested, but was in fact neither, his pretensions infuriated me. By force of will I would restrain my rage, because I was constantly aware that the object of the trial was not to persuade the judge but to persuade the twelve common folk in the jury box.

Outwardly, in front of the jury, I had to project an

image of respect, even deference, toward this judge who was out to convict my client. I knew that when Grosso ruled against me during the course of the trial, I must appear obedient, almost childlike, in my acceptance of his decision. If he reprimanded me for overstepping proper bounds, I would meekly accept this public chastisement, in the hope that the jury would interpret this as evidence of earnest submission rather than playacting to make a good impression.

"Before we get on with the first witness," Grosso said, "I'd like to see counsel in my chambers without the court reporter." He stood and left the courtroom and entered his chambers.

John and I followed the judge inside.

Grosso walked behind his desk as John and I entered, and began pacing back and forth. He was furious. "I can see by the way things are starting in this trial, Roehmer, that I'm going to wind up holding you in contempt," he said. "You've been needling me from the moment you stepped into my courtroom. Jabbing at me, punching me, every time you open your mouth. And I'll be goddamned," he shouted, "if I'm going to let you get away with it."

"You are out of your mind," I yelled back. "And you can do what you like with me. If you want to send me to prison for contempt, go ahead. But I can tell you this: I intend to break my ass to see that my client gets a fair trial. This case should have been dismissed. The only reason it wasn't is that you want it for your own agenda."

"Bullshit! I wouldn't dismiss it because this woman

went to that guy's apartment and coldly blasted the hell out of him."

"If there weren't front-page stories waiting for you in this trial, we wouldn't be here."

"You have no shame!" Judge Grosso said.

"Not over anything I've done or anything I'm going to do in this case. If you give my client a fair trial, she'll be acquitted. And if she doesn't get a fair trial, I'm going to make sure an appellate court will know it."

"You ungrateful bastard. You've been baiting me from the get-go. I have a good mind to hold you in contempt and send you to jail directly from here."

I pounded the judge's desk. "Try it," I said, looking him directly in the eye. "You're not going to intimidate me. The contempt you're talking about is in my mind, not in anything I've said or done in your courtroom. Is that all?"

"Get out of here," Judge Grosso said.

I stomped out of his chambers.

"What was that about?" Lisa asked as I returned to my seat next to her. "I could hear screaming going on in there."

"The guy's nuts. Absolutely paranoid."

"What did he say?"

"He said I've been taunting him from the moment I walked into this courtroom, that I've been trying to control the proceedings and belittle him." Of course I had been trying to control the proceedings. It's what every good lawyer tried to do in a trial. Grosso must have tried to do the same thing when he was a lawyer.

"Calm down, Michael," Lisa said.

"I'm calm. The little twerp. Don't worry, I'll control myself." I took a deep breath.

The fact that I was in love with Lisa was now jeopardizing her life. If I was too emotional to be objective, my competence as a lawyer was at risk. The irony was that I didn't want to represent monster clients, whom I hated but was so successful in defending, and here I was representing someone I cared for so much that I was apparently rendered unable to act in a professional manner in her behalf. I had to calm down.

"I won't lose control," I muttered to myself.

Chapter 26

JOHN LED THE state's first witness through his testimony the following morning. Lisa and I sat at our places at counsel table as the police officer described Betz's apartment.

"And where was the body found, Officer?" John asked.

"In the bedroom," the police officer said.

"Was there any evidence of a struggle? Was the room in disarray in any way?" John asked.

"No. It was very neat."

"Did you find any weapons in the apartment?"

"Just one. The gun. It had five spent shells and one live round left in the remaining chamber."

"Was there any other evidence in the room that you found and confiscated?"

"Yes. Two glasses half-filled with liquor. One of the glasses had the defendant's lipstick on it."

"Your witness," John said.

I leaned over and whispered to Lisa, "Were you wearing lipstick?"

Lisa thought for a moment. "Yes, I guess I was."

"Why were you wearing lipstick? You never wear lipstick."

"I really don't know why I put it on. But I did put some on just before going to his apartment."

"No questions," I said.

"Doctor, how many bullets were found in the body of the decedent?" John asked the next witness.

"Five," the doctor answered.

"In what parts of the body?"

"One in the head, two in the chest, and two in the abdomen."

"Were you able to tell at what distance the gun was fired from?"

"Yes. By the powder burns. The gun was fired at very close range."

"Mr. Roehmer?" John said.

I stood at counsel table. "Doctor, from your examination of the decedent, were you able to tell which bullet entered the body first?"

"No. That would be impossible to say," he replied.

"Doctor, did you examine the fingernails of the decedent?" This was the information the doctor had confirmed when he had called me in my office months ago.

"I found skin under the fingernails of three fingers of the right hand."

"Doctor, would it be consistent with that finding to conclude that the decedent had scratched the skin of someone else?"

"Yes. That would be the most likely explanation."

"Perhaps when he was violently pulling at the defendant's clothes in his attempt to rape her?"

"Objection," John said. "That would be sheer speculation."

"I'll withdraw the question," I said. "Thank you, Doctor."

"Mr. Cantor, after you examined the bullets removed from the decedent," John asked the next witness, "were you able to tell from which gun those bullets were fired?"

"Yes. From the gun seized at the scene of the crime," the man answered.

"Was there any mechanical malfunction in the revolver that would have prevented the firing of the last bullet in the chamber?"

"No. There was nothing wrong with the gun. The person who fired the gun must have just stopped pulling the trigger."

"The fingerprints on the gun matched those found on one of the glasses," the following witness testified.

"And were you able to tell whose fingerprints they were?" John asked.

"Yes. The fingerprints belonged to those of the defendant, Lisa Altman."

"Mr. Roehmer?" John said, turning to me.

"No questions," I said.

"The state calls Gene Carter," John said.

"What's he going to say?" I asked, leaning over to Lisa. I had not seen or thought about Gene Carter since I had gone to Lisa's rehearsal and watched him abuse her on the empty stage.

"I have no idea what he's doing here," Lisa said.

I looked to the rear of the courtroom and watched as Carter entered and walked with his cane down the center aisle toward the witness stand. He was sworn in and took his seat.

"At Miss Altman's first performance after the trial of Mr. William Betz, did you hear her say anything about Mr. Betz?" John asked.

"Yes," Gene Carter said.

"What did you hear her say?"

"As plain as day. She said she should have killed him. And that she'd kill him the next time."

Lisa stood. "That's a lie," she shouted.

"Quiet. I'll not tolerate another outburst," Judge Grosso said, pounding his gavel.

"I never meant that. He knows that," Lisa pleaded.

"Miss Altman, sit down," Judge Grosso said.

I pulled Lisa back into her seat.

"Your witness," John said.

"Did you say that?" I whispered, leaning over to Lisa. "Did you say anything like that? It's okay if you did. I can deal with it. But did you say it?"

"I wasn't serious. I was just upset," Lisa said.

I stood up. "Mr. Carter, how long have you worked with Miss Altman?" I asked.

"Six or seven years," Gene Carter answered.

"Would it be fair to say you've had many disagreements, even arguments, with her over the years?"

"Yes. I guess I would describe our relationship as bumpy. She's a wonderful dancer, let there be no mistake about that. Wonderful. World class."

"Mr. Carter, did you ever hear Miss Altman say things in anger?"

"Many times. She has quite a temper. You have to understand the enormous pressure on star performers. And they're especially anxious when they know there are only a limited number of years left in their careers."

"Has Miss Altman ever directed that anger at you?"

"Yes. Many times."

"Has she ever threatened you?"

"Yes."

"Threatened to kill you?"

"Yes."

"And has she ever?"

"Ever what?"

"Killed you?"

"Not yet."

The spectators in the back of the courtroom laughed.

"Thank you, Mr. Carter," I said.

Chapter 27

LISA SAID THAT for the sake of her sanity she needed to spend the nights during the trial alone in her apartment, and I understood that. She needed some quiet and solitude to be able to withstand the pressure in the courtroom. I would have preferred to share the nights with her, but I knew pushing her would be selfish, no matter how much I missed being with her.

The night after Gene Carter's testimony, I was alone in my study preparing for the next day, when Lisa would take the stand. I was sure it wasn't simply as a distraction or a break from my work that I found myself flipping through a file I kept in my desk that I had long ago marked "Personal."

I removed a copy of a letter I had written to Jenny more than twenty years before. We had been seeing each other for about six months, and she had given me a kind of autobiography her mother had written to her when Jenny was twelve. Jenny's mother had known she was dying and had wanted to give her daughter something of herself to hold on to after she was gone. Jenny had never shown it to anyone before she gave it to me.

I had labored over a response to Jenny, writing draft after draft, before sending her a letter. The letter in my file had been the last draft, typed by me and with words crossed out and handwritten changes written all over it. I read it:

Dearest Jenny,

The portrait of your mother was moving and lovely. While the facts were new, I somehow felt I already knew her by knowing you so well. Being privy to so personal a glimpse makes it tempting to offer a commentary, but because the glimpse is so incomplete, any conclusions would be presumptuous. What emerged was how much she would have enjoyed loving you as you are now. I'm not referring to the many interests she would have delighted in sharing with you—the people, ideas, music, books, etc.—they are obvious. But what I'm thinking of in particular is the passionate caring and involvement you bring to them, and the integrity with which you carry it all off. (Although I'd like to think your mother would have agreed with me that this integrity of yours is, at times, a pain in the ass.)

I sense that your mother would have had a strong empathy with a young woman who handles herself with your relentless honesty. Life without the honesty, well, you wouldn't consider it. "Wouldn't consider it!" you'd say with that marvelous wave of your hand. Your mother's compassion for people would no doubt have focused with very special attention and very special pride on you. It's evident from the way she led her life that she would have had a profound understanding of the fears and loneliness that that honesty at times entails. Your loss, among the many losses involved in her absence, is not now to have the benefit of her wisdom and her constant affirmation, her reassurance that you're right, absolutely right, in the most fundamental and important ways. I don't think your mother would have put you on any pedestal for it—she would have expected no less from her daughter; but she could not have hoped for more.

I understand how private these pages are to you, and so I return them to you now. They would have been returned earlier had I resigned myself sooner to so inadequate a response.

Love, Michael

Jenny had been very moved by my letter. This had, no doubt, been one of my goals in writing it. I wondered as I sat alone in my study why I always tried to find the worst motives in everything I did. The fact was that I had been genuinely knocked out by what Jenny's mother had written, and I had meant every word of my letter to Jenny—but I *had* wanted her to be moved by it.

I returned the letter to my "Personal" file and put the file back into the drawer of my desk.

Chapter 28

"THE DEFENSE CALLS Lisa Altman," I announced.

Everyone in the courtroom watched as Lisa stood and walked to the witness box. The court clerk held out a black Bible, and she placed her hand on it.

"Do you swear to tell the truth, the whole truth, and nothing but the truth?" the clerk asked.

"I do," Lisa said.

"Please take a seat. State your name and spell it for the court reporter," the clerk ordered.

"Lisa Altman. *L-I-S-A. A-L-T-M-A-N.*"

As I walked toward my witness, I looked over the rail and saw the woman who did the drawings for the local television station. She was working in pastels, and she was already well on her way with a dramatic picture of Lisa in the witness box.

I was determined to keep my direct examination as brief as possible. John would bring out all the lurid details. Then I would still have an opportunity on redirect examination to go back over the most important points of her testimony. On the strength of my redirect, I hoped to leave the most lasting impression on the jury.

"Miss Altman, did you know the decedent, William Betz?" I asked as my first question. I didn't want to ask the more typical questions about her background to introduce her to the jury. I was sure the jury was already well aware of who she was.

"Yes. I knew him."

"How was it that you knew him?"

"He was the man who had raped me before, and when he tried to do it again, I shot him." This was the answer Lisa had given me the dozens of times we had rehearsed the question—and she gave it now in the same soft tone and slow tempo we had prepared.

"How did you come into possession of the gun that you used to shoot him?"

"After he was acquitted on the rape charge, I was terrified. I knew he would come after me again. Then he called me. I wasn't surprised, but I was terrified."

"Where were you when he called you?"

"I was in Houston, appearing in *Swan Lake*. He called me at my hotel. He knew I was in Texas. He found out what hotel I was staying at."

"What did you do?"

"As I say, I wasn't surprised, but I was terrified. I went to a store. They have gun shops there. And I bought a gun and some bullets."

"When was the next time you saw Betz?"

"When I returned to New York. He called me again, several times. He said he wanted to see me. He said that he didn't want to rape me again, he wanted to worship me."

"What did you say to him?"

"I told him he was crazy. That he should leave me alone."

"And then what happened?"

"He called me again. He said if I didn't come over to his apartment, he'd come get me. If not that night, another night—he'd find me and force me to love him."

"What did you think when he said this to you?"

"I knew it was just a matter of time before he'd try to rape me again."

"What did you do?"

"I went to his apartment. I went there to plead with him, to threaten him, I don't know."

"You took your gun?"

"I wasn't going to use it. I was going to threaten him with it, to convince him to leave me alone."

"So you went to his apartment?"

"Yes."

"And then what happened?"

"He insisted we have a drink. We drank. He told me he would make me very happy. I told him he was crazy and to leave me alone."

"Yes?"

"I took the gun out of my handbag. I wasn't going to use it. He laughed. He laughed at me. He started to come toward me."

"Miss Altman, did you go to the apartment of William Betz with the intention of shooting him?"

"I did not. I swear it. I did not."

"When he was walking toward you, what were you thinking?"

"He was smiling. He had that crazed, fixed smile on his face."

"What were you thinking?"

"I knew he was going to rape me again, and I was terrified."

"Your witness," I said.

The first act was over. Lisa had been good, very good. The courtroom was dead silent. The jury had been hanging on her every word. Only Judge Grosso looked dubious as he sat there with his lips pursed like a man who had just tasted a lemon.

John stood and approached Lisa as I returned to my seat at counsel table.

"Miss Altman," John began, "you said you felt threatened by Mr. William Betz, and feared he might rape you again. Did you tell anybody of your anxiety before you went to his apartment and shot him?"

"No. I had no one to tell," Lisa said.

"Miss Altman, you could have called the police. Did you call the police?"

"No. I didn't think they would do anything about it."

"Miss Altman, you said you received threatening phone calls from Mr. Betz. Did you tell anybody about that before murdering him?"

"Objection," I shouted. "It wasn't murder, it was self-defense. Mr. Phalen knows the difference." I certainly wasn't going to let him slip that by. But I had shouted, and I hadn't needed to do that. It was clear to me that I was on a hair trigger. I told myself to calm down, calm down, damn it!

"Your Honor, it's for the jury to decide if they really believe it was self-defense," John said. "I'll rephrase the question. Did you tell anybody about the alleged phone calls before shooting Mr. Betz?"

"No. I didn't."

"Miss Altman, did you call the police about the phone calls?"

"No. They didn't help me the last time."

"Miss Altman, you claim that you bought the gun to protect yourself. Is that correct?"

"Yes. That's true."

"Did you plan on using it?"

"No. I had never fired a gun in my life. I thought if he ever came after me, pointing the gun at him would be enough."

"Then why did you buy the bullets?"

"I don't know. They sold them to me at the same time. The man at the gun store asked me, 'Do you want bullets?' And I said yes."

"Miss Altman, when you went to Mr. Betz's house, you knew there were bullets in the gun, didn't you?"

"Yes. That's where I kept the bullets. And it was good that I did. Pointing the gun at him was not enough. When I pointed the gun, he just kept coming at me."

John walked over to where I was sitting at counsel table. "That was good, Michael," John whispered. "You prepared her well."

"Thank you, John," I said, being careful not to smile, which would have looked bad to the jury.

John, standing behind me, turned back to Lisa. "You put five bullets into the man, didn't you?"

"I honestly don't know how many. I just kept firing."

"Miss Altman, I assume you are trying to tell this jury you were panicked, you didn't know what you were doing. Is that correct?"

"Yes. That's what happened."

"Then what happened to the sixth bullet?"

"What do you mean?"

"Miss Altman, if you were so panicked, why didn't you empty the gun and put the sixth bullet into him?"

"I don't know. I guess I just stopped. He had fallen to the floor. I guess I just stopped pulling the trigger."

"Isn't it a fact, Miss Altman, that you hated this man?"

"Yes. I hated him."

"And that you wanted to kill him for what he had done to you the last time you had been alone together?"

"I hated him. But I didn't go there to kill him. I didn't want to kill him. I just wanted him to stop tormenting me."

"Miss Altman, you wanted revenge, that's why you deliberately shot him. Isn't that a fact?"

"No. That's not a fact."

"When he came at you, he didn't have a weapon, did he?"

"No. He didn't have a weapon. He didn't have a weapon the last time he raped me, either."

"And before shooting him, you calmly, coolly had a drink with him, didn't you?"

"We had a drink. I wasn't at all calm. I was terrified. I was sitting across from the man who raped me, and who was threatening to rape me again."

"Your Honor, I have nothing more."

I stood and approached the witness. "Your Honor, I have a few more questions on redirect."

"You may proceed," Judge Grosso said.

"Miss Altman, at exactly what point did you actually shoot him?" I asked. "You said that he started toward you—did you shoot him then?"

"No. I told him to stop, to leave me alone. He just kept coming."

"Then what happened?"

"He lunged at me. He ripped my clothes. I ran backward, I remember, and when he started at me again that's when I shot him."

I walked over to counsel table and removed a torn, yellow silk blouse from a bag. I returned to Lisa and showed it to her.

"Do you recognize this?"

Lisa took the blouse and held it with both hands. She stared at it for a moment. "Yes. This was the blouse that I was wearing, the one that he ripped when he lunged at me."

"Did he scratch you when he ripped at your clothes?"

"Yes. He did. He scratched me on my stomach. I was so frightened that I didn't even realize that he had scratched me at the time. I didn't know that I was bleeding. I didn't feel any pain, I was so frightened."

I walked over to counsel table and removed an eight-by-ten color photograph from a folder. I returned to Lisa and showed her the photograph.

"Did you at my suggestion have a photograph taken of the scratches?"

"Yes."

I handed her the photograph. "Do you recognize this?"

"This is the photograph. It was taken three days after the shooting."

"Does it accurately reflect what the scratches looked like at that time?"

"Yes. It does." Lisa looked up at the jury. She looked intently at each juror, one at a time, just as I had told her to do.

"Your Honor," I said. "I would ask that this photograph be entered in evidence and passed around the jury."

"Let me see," Judge Grosso asked.

I handed the photograph to a court officer, who brought it to the judge. Grosso studied it, then handed it back to the court officer.

"It's admitted," Judge Grosso said, reluctantly. He had no choice. "Give it to the jury."

The court officer took the photograph of Lisa from Grosso, walked over to the first juror, and handed it to her.

I walked over to John. "You didn't think I'd forget, did you?" I whispered as the photograph was being passed around the jury.

"It didn't enter my mind that you would," John said.

After the photograph had finally snaked its way around to the last juror, it was handed back to the court officer.

"I have nothing further to ask the defendant," I said to the judge.

"Nothing further," John said.

Lisa started to step down from the witness stand.

"Just a second," Judge Grosso said. "I have a few questions."

Lisa returned to her chair in the witness box.

"Miss Altman," Judge Grosso said, "in the trial against William Betz, didn't your attorney, Mr. Roehmer, represent Mr. Betz?"

"Yes, he did."

"What's he up to?" I whispered to John, who was standing next to me.

"Beats me," John said.

"And didn't Mr. Roehmer cross-examine you in that trial where you claimed to have been raped by Mr. Betz?"

"Yes, he did," Lisa said.

"And didn't Mr. Roehmer get you to admit that you had met Mr. Betz prior to the time you claimed to have been raped by him?"

"The son of a bitch has gotten the transcript of the first trial," I said to John.

"He refreshed my recollection about that," Lisa said. "I hadn't really met him. He had bumped into me backstage."

"And by the way, Miss Altman," Judge Grosso said, "the jury concluded—no doubt, in part, because of Mr. Roehmer's searching cross-examination of you—that you hadn't been raped, isn't that correct?"

Lisa looked over to me for help.

"Objection," I shouted. "The jury concluded that the state hadn't proven its case beyond a reasonable doubt that Betz had committed the rape. That's all the jury concluded by its verdict. And there's even less evidence in this case that Miss Altman committed murder."

"Save your speech for the summation, Counselor," Judge Grosso said. "So, Miss Altman, I assume you learned a great deal from Mr. Roehmer's cross-examination of you in the first trial, that would have helped you to prepare for this trial, isn't that correct?"

"Objection," I shouted. "That is sheer speculation. There is no evidence to support that."

"Do you think so, Counselor? I guess that will be for the jury to decide. Answer the question, Miss Altman."

"That's just a grotesque lie," Lisa said.

"Your Honor, may counsel approach sidebar?" I insisted.

"Counselor, I am unaccustomed to being interrupted when I am asking questions of a witness," Grosso said.

"But Your Honor, I fear that irreparable injury may occur unless something is addressed immediately."

"Very well." Grosso motioned with his hand to summon the lawyers.

John and I walked to the side of the judge's desk. The court reporter detached her machine from its tripod and carried it with her to join us.

"Yes, Counselor," Grosso said. "This had better be good."

"As Your Honor knows," I said, "the prosecutor in

this case is very able. He has conducted a very extensive cross-examination."

"Of course. Get on with it, Counselor," the judge said, his impatience evident to everyone in the courtroom.

"Your Honor, with all due respect, I think you may be unaware that your questions seem clearly to be challenging the credibility of my client. The jury would interpret this as a second cross-examination, and a much more potent one simply because it is coming from someone who is supposed to be an impartial judge."

"I *am* impartial, and I do have the right to put questions to a witness, to test credibility or for any other reason."

"But when you were asking your questions, you were speaking in a tone that indicated that you didn't believe the answers the witness was giving, as if signaling to the jury that they shouldn't believe those answers either. The transcript of the record the court reporter is taking down won't show an appellate court the kind of subtle communication you have just made to the jury."

Judge Grosso bit his lower lip in anger. "Counselor, I don't want you muddying this record with your faulty perceptions. I know how I was speaking to this jury. I wasn't conveying my personal feelings. Isn't that right, Mr. Prosecutor?"

"Yes, sir," John obediently responded. It would have been too much to expect him to do otherwise.

Grosso's anger was clearly visible to the jury. "I can only assume that your ability to observe accurately has been impaired by your partisan zeal. Is there anything else, Counselor?"

Both Grosso and I knew that he was signaling to the jury that I had said something improper, and we both knew this would make the jury less sympathetic to me and my client. I decided I was willing to pay this price.

"Yes, sir," I pressed on. "In a similar vein, the transcript should reflect that when you began speaking to my client, you raised your eyebrow as if you were skeptical of whatever the witness would answer. I submit, Your Honor, that you were conveying to the jury in a manner which would not be reviewable from a cold transcript the impression that you did not think the jury should believe the defendant. It was as if you were saying you would be surprised if *anyone* believed the defendant."

"Counselor, I am getting tired of your personal attacks on me. Quite frankly, I find them contemptuous. I did not raise my eyebrow. I have not been communicating to the jury in some secret way. And I resent you filling this record with false and, I might say, paranoid accusations. Go back to your places, and if you have any further objections, make them when I have finished, when—as you know—it is the appropriate time to make all the objections you want."

John and I and the court reporter returned to our places.

"Let's see if that slows the son of a bitch down from totally burying me," I mumbled to myself as I sat down.

Judge Grosso stared at the witness for a moment. "You may step down, Miss Altman," he said.

Grosso was finished with Lisa. I had at least limited the damage.

Chapter 29

I WAS LEANING over the rail of the jury box as the jurors listened in rapt attention. "It would be more satisfying to all of us," I said in a near whisper, "if we could understand why a man like William Betz would torment this woman. Perhaps it was some perversion, or lust, or hatred of women—who knows? He may not have known himself. How much of the behavior in our own lives do we fully understand? He embraced some fantasy in which he would love and be loved by Miss Altman. It would be arrogant to think of ourselves as free spirits, unfettered by misdeeds done to us by others in our past. And no doubt William Betz had suffered such misdeeds or much worse in his past."

I paused for a moment. I looked back at Lisa and then returned to the jury.

"In trying to understand Betz's behavior or Lisa Altman's response to it, we are left in the end with too much that is unknown and unknowable. Who knows what generated or fed his fantasies? We would prefer to think of ourselves as having been born fully grown, without some invisible hand tugging strings tied to our limbs, strings that were tied when we were too young to notice. We become hardened by the small and large wounds suffered over a lifetime. Some of us become cynical; others try to make their lives bearable by constructing elaborate fantasies. At times, our actions are simply beyond our imperfect intelligence to comprehend."

I paused again. I looked over at Lisa, who was anxiously hanging on to my every word. She seemed like a frightened child. I turned back to the jury.

"Obviously he let Miss Altman into his apartment—there was no evidence of a break-in. Surely she didn't hold the gun on him to gain entry—they had a drink together, at his insistence. He welcomed her after threatening her if she wouldn't come. Miss Altman claims he attacked her. The torn blouse, the scars on her stomach, and the skin under his nails, are all proof of what she is saying.

"The law recognizes our limitations in divining motives or deeper explanations of behavior—in this case that of Betz or of my client. The only finding you must make is whether the state has proven its case against my client beyond a reasonable doubt. Given the lack of evidence of guilt and the substantial evidence of self-defense, you must have a reasonable doubt," I said as I concluded my summation. I stared at each juror, one at a time. Each person looked back at me, but I couldn't get any sense of whether they were at all persuaded by what I had said.

Chapter 30

I SAT ALONE on the wooden bench in the corridor outside the courtroom, waiting for the verdict. Lisa had insisted on remaining in the courtroom in her chair at counsel table. She had told me that she wanted to be alone.

I wasn't thinking about the jury's deliberation or the effect their verdict would have on Lisa's life. Instead, I thought about my own life. For years—surely up until my defense of the man who had raped Lisa—I'd had no difficulty separating myself from my clients. In some ways I had also been able to separate myself from aspects of my own behavior that I found distasteful. At times, I had even taken pride in my ability to keep so many things from touching me. But I had been paying a heavy price.

As I sat on the bench, I felt again as I often did when my work was done at the end of a trial: that all the air had seeped out of me. I took a quick inventory: the heaviness in my arms and shoulders, the effort in breathing, the beat of my pulse pounding in my left ear—I remembered all the symptoms as I had waited for the verdict in the Betz trial.

Yes, I'd had to adjust to the world I had been part of for the last twenty years. I had adjusted to the violence and the inhumanity. I had adjusted to the lies, the incompetence, and the brutality. Judge Bennett, it turned out, hadn't adjusted, and one day his head exploded.

I had experienced each trial up until this one with Lisa as merely a battle between adversaries, a battle in which trial lawyers were simply competitors. More often than not, I had wanted to win for my own sake, and had not really given a damn about the client. Winning a case had merely meant beating the other guy. A victory furnished a high like no other. That high had justified almost anything.

I had always seen a trial as a high-stakes contest: As a lawyer I was literally playing the game for someone's life. I had loved the role of rescuer—even when the person I rescued was despicable. Now, with a client I loved, I was having a hard time containing the desperation in my desire to win.

"How's it going?"

Startled, I looked up to see Cheryl Hazelton.

"I'm trying a case down the hall, and I saw you sitting here looking very lonely," she said.

"Have a seat, Cheryl. It's good to see you," I said.

"What are you up to, Michael?" Cheryl asked as she sat down beside me.

"The jury's out on my murder case."

"I'm still not used to waiting for verdicts—and murders are the worst."

I nodded.

"You know, Michael, I've often thought about the things you said at Bear's funeral. I was very moved by them."

"I miss him a lot."

"So do I," she said. "When I was first assigned to Bear's court, I was extremely conscious of his reputation—'the pit bull of justice,' that sort of thing—because of the way he tormented lawyers in front of jurors. So I was furious at the first assistant for putting me there."

"Sometimes he went too far, but it was because he really cared," I said.

"Before that I'd worked a year in the appellate section, writing briefs and arguing in front of judges who asked me polite academic questions raised by my appeals."

"So why did you move?"

"I wanted experience in front of juries. I wanted action. But I certainly didn't want to be thrown in with a judge who was a madman when I was fumbling through my first trials."

"It does seem a little cruel to have started you off with Bear," I said.

"I knew it wasn't because I was black—the first assistant prosecutor was also black. But I'm damn sure it was because I was a woman."

"You're probably right."

"But I was determined to make the best of it. I had convinced myself that Bear's brilliance would help me learn my craft more quickly. And as far as his meanness went, well, I'd decided I would have to deal with that. Damn! I grew up in Harlem; I should know how to survive a good street fight. And besides, one way or another I'd never had a problem getting men to come around."

"So how did it go?"

"My first trial was a fiasco. A fiasco! I didn't know where to stand, how to have the court reporter mark the documents, how to deal with the witnesses. Nothing!"

"Well, no one does in the beginning."

"But I really didn't know anything. And Bear was worse than no help. He sat up there on his bench, glaring down at me, fuming with impatience."

"He was like that with everyone when they were first starting out."

"I remember at one point he slapped his hand down on his desk and yelled at me for wasting time. When I tried to go on asking the defendant questions, Bear interrupted me to put his own questions, and when he had finished, he ordered me to sit down.

"Well, I tell you, it was the best way to learn. Maybe it wasn't the most pleasant way to do it, but you really learned to prepare a case.

"Christ, I used to be in my office till midnight studying upper-court opinions, going over the testimony with witnesses, reviewing the evidence, making sure I knew exactly what I'd be doing the next day. I swore I'd never give him another chance to abuse me the way he did in my first trial with him."

"Well, there you go. Although after all this I'm not really sure why you liked the guy."

"Michael, I didn't like the guy. I loved him."

"Loved him?"

"Loved him. I thought you knew," Cheryl said.

I shook my head.

"Remember the case we had together when I lost the heroin?"

"Of course."

"After he threw the case out, I went to see him in his chambers. When I was alone with him, I told him that I felt humiliated, and that I was going to quit the prosecutor's office and maybe even give up being a lawyer altogether."

"I knew you were terribly upset."

"When I began to cry, Bear put his arms around me to calm me down. The two of us stood together for a few minutes. When I finally stopped sobbing, he kissed me."

I nodded, but I'd had no idea.

"He often spoke to me about his marriage to Margaret. He called it . . . he would say, 'On balance, a perfectly sensible marriage.' He knew that it would be a terrible scandal if his relationship with an assistant prosecutor became public—it would probably have forced his resignation. But somehow he was confident that no one would suspect anything. Maybe it was arrogance, or just plain wishful thinking, to believe we had managed to keep our secret, but we took some precautions: we only saw each other in his chambers or in my apartment. In court he treated me like anyone else. I guess we were just lucky."

"I guess *you* miss him, too."

She nodded.

Chapter 31

THE COURTROOM WAS crowded with spectators and the press. John was on one side of counsel table; I was on the other side, next to Lisa. A court officer stood behind us. The court stenographer was ready at her machine. Judge Grosso was on the bench. And the clerk was standing at his desk.

The jurors filed in from the jury room and took their seats in the jury box.

"Madam forelady, has the jury reached a verdict?" the clerk asked.

The forelady stood, a piece of paper shaking in her hand. "We have," she said.

"Madam forelady, is that verdict unanimous?" the clerk asked.

"It is," the woman said.

"Please hand your verdict sheet to the court attendant," the clerk said.

A court officer walked over to the forelady, took

the piece of paper from her, crossed the floor, and handed it to the judge.

Judge Grosso took the paper and read it. His face gave no clue as to what the verdict was. He handed the paper back to the court officer, who carried it back to the forelady.

"Will the defendant stand, face the jury, and listen to the verdict," Judge Grosso said.

Lisa and I stood and faced the jury. I was more nervous than I'd ever been before as I waited for the answer. I looked over at Lisa. Her face seemed frozen, hardened, as if to withstand the blow of terrible news.

"How say you by your verdict?" Judge Grosso asked. "Is the defendant, Lisa Altman, guilty or not guilty of the charge of murder?" Having seen the verdict sheet, Grosso was the only person in the courtroom, other than the jurors, who knew the answer.

The forelady cleared her throat. "We the jury," she said, "find the defendant not guilty."

Some of the spectators gasped. Several reporters ran out of the courtroom on their way to telephones.

Lisa allowed a slight smile.

"Members of the jury," the clerk said, "you have said through your forelady that you find the defendant, Lisa Altman, not guilty of murder, and so say you all."

The jurors nodded.

"The jury is excused with the thanks of this court. You may return now to the jury control room," Judge Grosso said.

The jurors stood and filed out of the jury box. Some of them smiled and some nodded at Lisa as they walked past her. She watched the jurors leave the courtroom.

Judge Grosso glared at me. "Well, you won this one, Mr. Roehmer. I'll see you next time." He stood and stormed into his chambers.

John approached me. We shook hands.

"Well done, Michael," John said.

"Thank you, John."

"I can't say I was surprised by the verdict. I'm sorry I had to leave it to a jury, but you understand," John said.

"Of course," I said. "You had no choice."

"Well, in the end, it's just as well," John said. "See you on that armed robbery in a couple of weeks." He gave a little wave and left the courtroom.

I turned to Lisa and smiled.

"Congratulations, Michael," Lisa said. "You did a great job. As I knew you would."

"Thank you. I'm relieved," I said, and started to put my arm around her. "Relieved for both of us."

"I'm glad you are," she said. She seemed to stiffen from the touch of my arm across her shoulder, so I pulled it back.

"Now that this ordeal is over, we can finally talk about us," I said.

"Tell me, Michael, do you feel you've redeemed yourself?"

"What do you mean?"

"Do you finally feel freed of your guilt for what you did to me in the first trial?"

I studied Lisa. "Maybe so," I said.

"The prosecutor feels better, too, don't you think?" Lisa asked.

"I guess so."

"All neat and tidy, isn't it, Counselor?"

"So it seems."

"Right. Michael, I need some time alone. I'll call you in a few days."

Lisa stood and walked out of the courtroom.

I remained at my seat at counsel table for a moment, dumbfounded. Finally, I slowly began to gather my papers.

"What's wrong, Michael?" the court clerk asked.

"Nothing. Nothing's wrong," I said.

"Congratulations," he said. "Here's your exhibits." He handed me the torn yellow blouse and the photograph of Lisa showing her scratches.

I nodded. "Thanks."

"That was a nice win, Michael. You don't lose many of them."

"Thank you."

"I see some lawyers come in here, time after time, they don't know what a 'not guilty' verdict sounds like. Not that they don't try to win. Lord knows, they try everything. You're just better than they are."

"Thank you."

"It makes such a difference," the clerk said.

"What's that?"

"Having an innocent client. It justifies all the bullshit built into the system."

"An innocent client? Yes, I guess so," I said.

I don't remember what I said to the reporters who were waiting in the corridor outside the courtroom.

Chapter 32

THE NIGHT AFTER the verdict I was at home sitting in the comfortable stuffed chair in my study. I picked up a law journal and flipped through the pages. I quickly realized that the last thing I wanted to do was read about the law. I threw the journal on the table beside me.

I got up from my chair and put on the videotape I had made of Molly's last birthday party. I watched the children playing and hopping like bunnies on the floor of the room just outside my study. That was almost six months ago. It was odd to recall that as I was filming that scene Lisa had been outside the house, waiting and watching. So much had happened since then.

"Why don't you put the camera down," I could hear Jenny telling me on the tape, as I kept filming. Someday Molly would enjoy watching these tapes, I thought, although she'd never see me on them, since I was always behind the camera.

I wondered what it would be like if I had tapes of me with my parents when I was a young man. Would my mother be as warm and lovely as I remembered her, and my father as strong and solid as I pictured him now? I couldn't summon up an image of myself when I was Molly's age. I would have been intrigued to see and hear a tape of our family when I was her age.

I wondered if in fact Molly would ever take the tapes of herself to a shrink, as I had often joked she would one day.

I put on a different tape. I had made this one the day before Molly's third birthday. Jenny and Molly were in the kitchen baking chocolate chip cookies. Both of them were wearing pretty aprons with bright printed flowers on them. Molly had white baking powder all over her apron and on her face and hair. She and her mother were both giggling. We were all happy then, or at least I had thought so. There was nothing on the tape to give a clue that the day after the birthday party, just two days after the scene I was watching on the tape, Jenny was going to tell me she was leaving me. Jenny was laughing! Where was the evidence?

I turned off the tape. How could I be so perceptive in my professional life in the courtroom and so obtuse in my personal life? My good friend from law school, Charles, whom I hardly ever saw anymore, had once told me that I was eager to shoot videos of Molly so that I would be giving myself the best defense. But the truth was that the videos were not exculpatory. They were an indictment, proof that I had totally missed what was really going on in front of my eyes.

I went upstairs. As I passed Molly's room I noticed that her light was still on. I opened the door and entered the room. She was in her bed, leafing through a large picture book.

"Hi, sweetheart," I said.

"Hi, Daddy." She smiled at me, with a smile that would have melted the heart of a snowman.

"You should be asleep. It's past nine." I walked over to her and sat down on her bed.

"I'm having a little trouble going to sleep."

I asked her if she remembered when I used to sing her to sleep.

"I sure do, Daddy," my darling four-year-old daughter said.

"Hush, little baby, don't say a word," I began to sing, "Papa's going to buy you a mockingbird. And if that mockingbird don't sing, Papa's going to buy you a diamond ring."

"Yes, I remember. It was when I was a little baby," Molly said, suddenly sounding quite old.

"I used to love to sing to you," I said.

"I know, Daddy."

"I knew very few songs."

"I know, Daddy."

"Did you like the song about the mockingbird?" I asked.

"No," she said. "I guess I really didn't like it very much."

"You didn't? How come?"

"I always thought it was very sad. Things kept breaking or getting lost."

"Why didn't you ever tell me? I always thought you loved it."

"I knew you liked to sing it, and I didn't want to hurt your feelings."

I was very touched. At four years Molly was more sensitive and considerate than I often was at my ripe old age. "You should know you can tell me whatever you're feeling, sweetheart," I said, and kissed her good night.

As I was walking out of her room, Molly said, "Daddy, I've been missing you."

"I've missed you, too," I said. "I was very busy with a case, but that's over, and I'm home now."

I walked back to the bed. I scooped Molly up into my arms and hugged her tightly. "You're the most precious and dearest thing in the world to me," I said as I held her in my arms.

"I love you too," she said.

When Molly rested her head again on the pillow, we smiled at each other for a few moments. I stared at my darling daughter, and I thought how peaceful and innocent she seemed. I had tried so hard over the years to make her life as perfect and secure as I could. I had scrupulously sheltered her from the harshness of the life I moved in. Of course, I told her nothing of the violence and the lies. I never told her about death. I had done everything I could to limit her awareness of such things. At some point, soon enough, she would learn all about the world's tragedies. Now, as I looked into Molly's vulnerable and trusting face, I wondered how long it was wise to wait before telling her about how people could be cruel to one another.

"Daddy, why are you crying?"

"Am I crying?" I asked. "I guess I was thinking about how glad I am that we're together. I suppose I'm being silly. You should go to sleep, and so should I."

I kissed Molly on the forehead again. I got up from the bed, turned off her light, and went to bed.

Chapter 33

I DIDN'T HEAR from Lisa for days.

I had been totally unprepared for the anger I sensed behind her question about whether the acquittal had freed me from guilt. Here I was, a professional who made a living out of quick responses and could think on his feet faster than anyone else, and I had no answer. I could find no "objection" to her attack on me. I had simply been totally unprepared.

Everyone had congratulated me on the verdict. Even Jenny had called me.

And when I returned to my office the following week, Sylvia did the unthinkable and told me she was proud of me.

When I sat at my desk, I just stared straight ahead. I sat like that for several minutes. I didn't have the interest or the energy to focus on a new case.

Finally, I got up and walked over to the table where I'd thrown the accordion file containing the evidence

I had submitted in Lisa's trial. I brought the file back to my desk. I removed the photograph showing Lisa's wounds. This had been the single most important piece of evidence in saving Lisa's life. If there had been physical evidence like this photograph or the torn blouse in the trial against Betz, I would have probably lost that trial, and Betz would still be alive.

I stared at the photograph. The most crucial contribution I had made to Lisa's acquittal had probably been my insistence that she have that picture taken. I reached into my desk drawer and pulled out a magnifying glass. I held the glass over the part of the photograph that showed the scratches. There were three narrow furrows, each about four inches long— reddish brown gashes that were already starting to heal, beginning just under the rib cage and running straight down to the middle of her stomach.

I pulled the yellow silk blouse from the folder and spread it out on my desk. I stared at it for a moment. I bent forward to smell the blouse, but I detected no odor. I buttoned it up the front. All the small pearl buttons were still intact above and below the wide horizontal tear across the front. I folded the blouse and arranged it neatly on my desk like a blouse on a shelf in a store, lining the upper and lower torn halves up with each other.

I stared at the three bloodstains running down the front of the blouse. The stains radiated out like drops spreading on an ink blotter, leaving three columns that were almost wide enough to touch each other. The upper half of the blouse where the stains began lined up perfectly with the bottom half of the torn blouse where the columns of bloodstain continued.

I looked again at the photograph. The wounds matched in length, width, and location where the stains appeared on the blouse. That was the problem. They matched too perfectly. How could she have bled like that *before* the blouse was torn?

Chapter 34

SHE MERELY NODDED at me when I opened the door to her dressing room at the theater. She didn't seem at all surprised to see me. She was seated at her dressing table in front of the mirror. It was after a rehearsal, like the first time I had been in that room.

"You ripped the blouse yourself, didn't you?" I asked as I stepped inside the room.

She just watched me and waited.

"Grosso was more right than he realized," I said.

"What do you mean?" she asked.

"I mean you learned a great deal from me in the first trial," I said.

"You're a better teacher than you realized," Lisa said.

"All it took you was a few scratches from a dead man's hand to convince me that he had tried to rape you again."

"What makes you so sure?"

"The stains on the upper and lower halves of the blouse were continuous. To get that kind of pattern in the stains, the blouse would have to be torn after you got the wounds."

"His mouth and eyes were open," she said without emotion. "I took each finger, one at a time, and made the scratches. I buttoned the blouse and blotted it against myself. I tore the blouse when I got home."

"So this was revenge. You murdered him for what he did to you before?" I asked.

"He could have tried to rape me, Counselor. I could have shot him in self-defense and found it necessary to do something to make the jury believe me this time."

"Is that what happened?"

"You've got to admit that my having those scratches this time around made a big difference in the cross-examination."

"And the call to the prosecutor? That was you pretending to be another woman who had been raped by Betz?"

"I could have done that to secure a cheap bail even if I were innocent."

I stared at Lisa, trying to find in her face some clue to what she was thinking. It was as if she were a total stranger, as if we had not spent hundreds of hours together, eaten meals together, made love together, slept together, talked endlessly. I didn't know this woman at all.

Lisa smiled. "How would you feel if I told you this wasn't a revenge murder because he didn't rape me even the first time?"

"That never occurred to me."

"Well, those are the two options. Which would soothe your conscience more? Would you feel better believing that he was guilty in the first trial?"

"I don't know," I said.

"Tell me when you decide."

"Then what?"

"I'll tell you the answer you want to hear."

"And our relationship? What was all that about?"

"It was nothing personal. I needed you to represent me, and I was sure you'd do a better job if you loved me."

"I can't believe you could be that calculating."

"Oh come on, Michael, we're not that different. I was no more calculating, no more a performer, than you've been all your life."

"You're that cold?"

"We're both professionals, remember? Maybe when I get older, I'll suffer little pangs of guilt like you."

I watched Lisa shove some things into her tote bag. She nodded at me and left.

Suddenly I was alone in Lisa's dressing room. She had just used some of my own language about my detachment from "monster clients" to explain her behavior with me. The irony was not lost on me. She must have been waiting for months to throw some of those phrases back in my face.

I couldn't accept the fact that she had hated me so much for so long. If I was capable of being such a good judge of a witness on the stand, how could I have been so blind for so long in such an intimate relationship?

The image of the young lawyer I had seen months before in the lawyers' conference room of the jail came to mind. I remembered my condescending observation about how naive he sounded—when he had simply wanted to be reassured by his client that he'd been telling him the truth. I had not only stopped looked for that kind of reassurance a long time ago, but I must have also stopped looking for the truth altogether, it seemed. How else could I have been so blind?